"Put your arms around my neck," Jack commanded her as he linked his arms tightly around Colleen's waist.

There was really nowhere else for her arms to go, she realized dizzily. They were so close that there wasn't an inch of her not touching him, yet somehow he pressed even closer. Colleen could feel the solid, muscular heat of him imprinted against the length of her whole body; she cold feel his breath in her hair.

"Relax," Jack said softly. "You need to loosen up."

"I'm not a very good dancer. I keep worrying I'll end up crippling my partner by stepping all over his feet." Her words were prophetic, for at that moment the high heel of her shoe nearly punctured his foot, but Jack deftly moved out of range. "See what I mean?" Colleen asked.

She waited for him to razz her about having two left feet. The last thing she expected was for him to cup the nape of her neck with his hand and begin a slow massage with his fingers.

"You're doing fine," he murmured, his other hand beginning to knead the sensitive hollow of her spine. Colleen felt every nerve responding to his sensuous caresses, as if her body had just burst into flames. . . .

WHAT ARE *LOVESWEPT* ROMANCES?

They are stories of true romance and touching emotion. We believe those two very important ingredients are constants in our highly sensual and very believable stories in the *LOVESWEPT* line. Our goal is to give you, the reader, stories of consistently high quality that may sometimes make you laugh, sometimes make you cry, but are always fresh and creative and contain many delightful surprises within their pages.

Most romance fans read an enormous number of books. Those they truly love, they keep. Others may be traded with friends and soon forgotten. We hope that each *LOVESWEPT* romance will be a treasure—a "keeper." We will always try to publish

LOVE STORIES YOU'LL NEVER FORGET
BY AUTHORS YOU'LL ALWAYS REMEMBER

The Editors

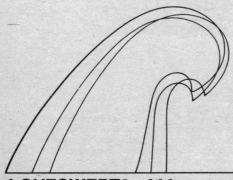

LOVESWEPT® • 444

Barbara Boswell
The Last Brady

 BANTAM BOOKS
NEW YORK • TORONTO • LONDON • SYDNEY • AUCKLAND

THE LAST BRADY

A Bantam Book / January 1991

*LOVESWEPT® and the wave device are registered
trademarks of Bantam Books, a division of
Bantam Doubleday Dell Publishing Group, Inc.
Registered in U.S. Patent
and Trademark Office and elsewhere.*

*If you would be interested in receiving protective vinyl
covers for your Loveswept books, please write to this
address for information:*

> Loveswept
> Bantam Books
> P. O. Box 985
> Hicksville, NY 11802

ISBN 0-553-44084-5

Published simultaneously in the United States and Canada

Bantam Books are published by Bantam Books, a division
of Bantam Doubleday Dell Publishing Group, Inc. Its trademark, consisting of the words "Bantam Books" and the
portrayal of a rooster, is Registered in U.S. Patent and
Trademark Office and in other countries. Marca Regis-
trada. Bantam Books, 666 Fifth Avenue, New York, New
York 10103.

PRINTED IN THE UNITED STATES OF AMERICA

OPM   0 9 8 7 6 5 4 3 2 1

One

_____

"Hey, Jack, Kazorowski wants to see you in his office right away."

Jackson Blackledge didn't glance away from the screen of his word-processing terminal, and his fingers didn't miss a letter as they moved nimbly over the keyboard. "Later, kid," he muttered to the eager young man he recognized as a part-time college intern. Skip Something or other. "Now, get lost. I'm on a roll here."

"Kazorowski says it's really important." An anxious note had crept into Skip's voice. Everybody at the _Buffalo Times-Gazette_ knew about Blackledge's temper, which was as unpredictable and explosive as a volcano.

"Has war been declared?" Jack demanded, pausing to glare at the young messenger. "Have the Buffalo Bills been sold to another city?"

"Uh, no, but—"

"Well, then, it's not really important, is it?" Blackledge returned his attention to the keyboard, unmistakably signaling dismissal to the hapless gofer.

Who refused to be dismissed. "I'm sorry, Jack, but Kazorowski _assigned_ me to bring you to his office. What the heck—" the young man's voice became wheedling. "I've already broken your concentration anyway, haven't I?"

Jack rose slowly from his chair, drawing himself to his full height, six feet, two inches of solid muscled masculinity. He slammed his palms down on his desk, watching the intern's ingenuous smile falter a bit.

Jack was fully aware of his intimidating physical presence; During his days as a professional athlete, he'd often used his size to psych out the opposition. He glanced at the short, rail-thin kid and then heaved a sigh. He wasn't on the ball field now. He was in the newsroom and young Skip was only doing his job, like every other working stiff in the place. "Lead the way, kid. I'll give Kazorowski ten minutes."

Skip smiled broadly, his relief palpable. "Only you can get away with laying down the law to the managing editor, Jack. I mean, he's everybody's boss, but you don't let *him* boss *you.* You call your own shots. I admire you for that, Jack."

"Yeah, I'm a regular role model. Only don't tell Kazorowski that you want to be like me. He thinks I'm a curse from heaven, and his ulcer couldn't handle the thought of two of us."

They walked through the newsroom, which was alive with midmorning activity. Some reporters sat at terminals working on stories, others were talking on telephones or shuffling through piles of mail. A small group was gathered at the coffee and soft-drink machines in the narrow corridor. At the back of everything was the city room proper.

Inside, Tom Kazorowski, overweight, balding, and looking much older than his fifty years, was smoking. A half-empty pack of cigarettes lay on his desk.

"You smoke way too much, Kaz," Jack observed, as he entered the office. "You know what your doctor said. Do you want to land back in the hospital?"

"If you're so concerned about my health, you can

do me a big favor and spare me the scene I know we're about to have," Kazorowski shot back.

"Uh-oh." Jack tensed. He walked to the small window and looked out. There wasn't much of a view. The building that housed the *Buffalo Times-Gazette* was in one of the oldest and most dilapidated parts of the city. The building itself, home to the *T-G* since its inception nearly seventy-five years ago, was as aged and run-down as the area.

September was a pretty time of year in western New York; the leaves were just beginning to change colors, and the summer greenery and flowers still flourished. But the dingy alley below Kazorowski's window was gloomy and forbidding, devoid of any seasonal beauty.

Jack turned to face the editor with one of his notorious Black Jack stares, steady and unwavering. "Give me the bad news, Kaz. No, let me guess— the publisher censored my column *again*."

Kazorowski was lighting a new cigarette from the smoking butt of his old one. "Nothing like that. Thank heaven." He cleared his throat. "Jack, I want to talk about your syndication deal. . . ."

"What about it?" His tone was belligerent, his dark eyes challenging.

"Of course, it's a real coup for a homegrown Buffalo columnist—and one affiliated with our paper— to be nationally syndicated in two hundred and twelve papers," Kaz said quickly. "Other cities have local columnists who've made it nationally, but you're the first and only for Buffalo! The *T-G* brass are whooping for joy. We're all hoping your new-found fame will help boost circulation, Jack. It's damn tough being the only afternoon daily and watching our circulation decline as people turn more and more to TV news."

Jack eyed him warily. "But—" he said. There had to be a but. He knew that Kazorowski never piled on the praise without some ulterior motive.

The editor took a deep breath. "Jack, you've been

contracted to write three columns a week for the syndication market, but the *T-G* needs five columns a week."

"Sorry, Kaz. One reason why I jumped at the syndication deal was because I've been writing five columns a week for the past five years. I want to cut down to three and gear them toward a national audience rather than a local one."

"But your column has been a smash here because of the local angle, Jack. I can understand your ambitions to write for the national market, but our readers want somebody local commenting on Buffalo news, gossip, and humor."

"So you want three columns a week suitable for national publication and two a week concentrating on the local scene? Jeez, Kaz, you don't ask for much. You don't pay much, either," Jack added dryly.

"The *T-G* isn't unreasonable, Jack. We understand the pressure your new syndication contract puts on you. That's why we—I—er—took the liberty of hiring you an assistant."

Jack stared at him. "A what?"

"You know, someone to help out. To eventually sort of take over the Tuesday and Thursday columns—under your tutelage and byline, of course," he added quickly. "We'd never hire someone who would compete with you. The column will keep your name."

"It's cheaper that way," Jack said, grimacing. "You couldn't afford to hire another columnist."

"Well, there is that . . ." Kaz attempted a smile. He prided himself on his frugality. "Jack, getting back to your assistant. All you have to do is—"

"Train some kid fresh out of journalism school how to write a readable column? Prepare myself for endless rewrites and pep talks? Hell, Tom, I'll spend more time wet-nursing him than I will writing my own columns."

"Her," Kazorowski interjected, fiddling a pencil.

"Huh?"

"Her. Your assistant. She's female, Jack."

Jack laughed. "C'mon, Kaz, quit joking around. Women write about food, weddings, and babies, or pop psychology and celebrities if they're less domestically oriented. I write columns about sports and politics and issues. I do satire and some serious stuff, but—"

"Lots of women read your column, Jack."

"Well, sure. But that doesn't mean one is qualified to *write* it. If you want a female columnist, put her on the women's pages and let her write about the adventures of picking a preschool or the latest diet craze or the ten most effective ways to flirt. Stuff like that."

"You're a dyed-in-the-wool sexist, Jack. No wonder every woman at the paper turned down the offer to work as your assistant."

Jack's eyes, black as onyx, black as the prefix of his surname, widened. "*Every one*?"

"None of the men on staff wanted the job, either," Kaz added. "The older writers are already established, and the younger ones don't want to play second fiddle or whipping boy to a notoriously difficult"—he cleared his throat—"would tyrant be the word I'm looking for?"

"Tyrant? Me?" Jack was offended. "True, I stand up for myself, but—"

"Some would describe you differently—using words like *domineering* and *confrontational*."

"What I am is self-assured. Confident."

"Jack, you crossed the line from confident to arrogant years ago."

"I'm a risk taker," Jack said grimly. "I make my own rules and refuse to suck up to anybody, including the so-called powers that be."

"And people looking for career security want to put a safe distance between themselves and you. That's why I had to go outside the paper to find you an assistant. I had to look outside Buffalo, actually.

You're something of a local legend in the newspaper business, Jack."

Kazorowski visibly braced himself for the explosion he was certain would follow.

In fact, Jack was about to work himself into a rage when he recalled that he'd just been described as confrontational. Kazorowski was obviously *expecting* him to blow up. The one thing Jack hated more than the idea of a bubble-headed female assistant ghostwriting his column twice a week was being viewed as predictable.

He smiled instead. It might not have been the type of smile that encouraged one to return it, but it was a smile nonetheless. "Tell me about this assistant you had to scour the country to find, Tom," he said sweetly. "I can already guess a few things—she's naive enough to accept a salary that's unconscionably low, even in this business."

"Boy, that's the truth!" Kazorowski rubbed his hands together. "You know how tight money is around here. In all honesty, working with you wasn't the *only* reason everybody turned down the job. The salary we offered was very low. We were afraid we'd have to raise it, and then I got this kid's résumé. I read some samples of her work and interviewed her. She's good, Jack. I was prepared to give her a song and dance about the notoriously low wages paid in the newspaper business, but she agreed to take the job immediately. At our price!"

"Do you think she's a rich little girl working for fun while living off the big, generous trust fund her daddy has set up for her?" Jack's dark eyes narrowed with sudden interest. And intent.

"Sorry to disappoint you, Blackledge, but if this girl is rich, I'll personally write those two columns a week myself for free. She doesn't look rich, doesn't sound or act rich. I'm sure she's just a middle-class kid with a nice suburban daddy and mommy who are straining their own budget to help their little girl begin her career."

"At least you could've hired me a wealthy deb on the make," Jack said, somewhat seriously.

"Still planning to marry for money?" Kaz grinned. "Good luck. You'll need it." Jack shrugged. "I married for what's known as love once and that was a total bust. Next time—if there ever is a next time—I'm definitely going for the bucks. Big bucks and a rich bride."

For just a moment, a shadow crossed Jack's face and the look of cynical indifference changed to one of disillusionment.

"Here's a sample of her work." Kazorowski's voice roused Jack from an unpleasant reverie.

He quickly glanced down at the paper the editor had handed him. "This is a how-I-spent-my-summer-vacation piece. You hired her on the basis of *this*?"

"Read it through. It's cute. Humorous. Definitely shows promise. She worked at Disney—"

"You hired a Mouseketeer to write my column?"

"She worked at Disney World during her college summer vacations—they hire people to dress like the cartoon characters and go around the park and mingle with visitors," Kaz explained patiently. "She was one of Donald Duck's nephews."

Jack rolled his eyes. "Terrific. I'm supposed to allow an ex-duck to write under my byline. Level with me, Kaz. Is she perky? Full of spunk and irrepressible charm?"

Kaz coughed. "Jack, for goodness' sake—"

"She is! You know how much I loathe perky and spunky. No way, Kazorowski. I'll write the columns myself. It'll be a pain in the ass, but anything beats having to deal with a birdbrain—and I use that term quite literally under these circumstances—who is—"

"She's been hired, and she starts tomorrow," Kaz interrupted. "She's had over a year of newspaper experience with papers in Houston and D.C., so she's not completely green. Hiring her was a good move, Jack. I don't intend for her to work exclusively with you. The entertainment and food editors have been begging for someone, and the three of you can share her. We've hired three people for the cost of less than one!"

"You're one helluva guy, Kaz." Jack shook his head, both disgusted and amused. "You're cheap *and* sly. But I'm giving you advance warning that I intend to do everything in my power to make her refuse to work with me."

The telephone rang and Kaz picked it up, clearly pleased to end the encounter.

Jack headed toward the door. "When she arrives here tomorrow, send her over to my place. I'm going to be working at home." His personal computer and a modem enabled him to do so, though he usually preferred coming in to work at his desk in the newsroom. Not tomorrow, though. He had a pest to scare off, and what better place than in the privacy of his own home.

Kaz covered the mouthpiece of the telephone and bellowed, "Jack, I'm not sending a twenty-three-year-old woman over to your place. You'll meet her here in the newsroom and then everybody will be safe from a sexual-harassment suit."

"Twenty-three?" Jack hit his forehead with the palm of his hand. "That makes her ten years younger than I am! *Ten years!* When I was starting puberty, she was starting nursery school, when I was learning to drive, she was learning to read! Kaz, this is ridiculous! I—"

"She'll be here at seven sharp, Blackledge."

"All right, I'll be here to meet her," Jack snapped. He'd lost this round, but he wasn't about to concede defeat. "And what's the eager little duckling's name?" His smile was diabolical.

Kaz looked uneasy. "Colleen Brady," he said, and returned to his phone call with a trouble frown.

*   *   *

Colleen Brady arrived in the newsroom of the *Buffalo Times-Gazette* at six-thirty. She was so eager to begin her first day on the job, she'd had to restrain herself from arriving an hour earlier.

Friendly staffers in the newsroom introduced her around as she waited for Jackson Blackledge to arrive. She'd been worried that the staff might resent an outsider winning the plum job of assistant to an important nationally syndicated columnist. That she would actually be permitted to write columns—under Mr. Blackledge's expert guidance—was simply a dream come true. It wouldn't have surprised her if some had shown jealousy or open hostility shown toward her.

To her surprise, everyone was warmly welcoming. She was handed a cup of coffee from the machine in the hall. As she took a sip and tried to choke back a cough, somebody made a joke about the potency of the dark, thick brew. Colleen joined in the laughter, making a mental note to bring her own coffee in a thermos from now on.

"He's here," someone whispered. "Black Jack has been spotted getting off the elevator."

Colleen came to attention. Mr. Blackledge wrote his columns under the pseudonym Black Jack.

There was an undercurrent of voices, some snickers, some sidelong glances at Colleen. She didn't understand exactly what was going on, but she'd been a newcomer and the outsider often enough in her life to know that it was all part of the game. The in crowd always had its jokes, language, and code. She knew from experience that the worst thing she could do would be to ask for information.

So Colleen, cautious and observant by nature, pretended to be oblivious to the sudden excitement in the air while she sipped the eye-popping coffee. Unfortunately, she wasn't facing the elevators, so unless she turned completely around, she couldn't see anyone entering the newsroom.

She opted against turning around. Too obvious.

It was always better not to ruin the group's anticipation of . . . of what? Colleen wasn't sure, but it was clear they were anticipating something. She continued her conversation with one of the junior reporters, pretending unconcern.

"Hey, Blackie, she's here!" called one of the sportswriters in a singsong voice. "Your new assistant is ready and waiting for you."

Colleen felt her cheeks begin to color. The man had made the neutral and harmless word *assistant* sound positively lewd!

"Okay, where is she?" sounded a rough, hard voice edged with impatience and anger.

"Right over there, Black Jack," came the ominously gleeful reply. "The cute little blonde."

Colleen set the coffee cup down on the corner of a desk and permitted herself to turn around slowly.

Jack Blackledge stood a few feet in front of her. He noticed her immediately, of course. She was the only stranger in the city room—and she was indeed a "cute little blonde."

His eyes flicked over her. Worn soft and loose, her pale blond hair was slightly longer than shoulder-length. She had impossibly big brown eyes, a sweet mouth that looked soft and sexy and temptingly mobile, and a peaches-and-cream complexion that was as smooth and flawless as fine porcelain.

"Are you Colleen Brady?" he demanded, buying time. He was caught off guard, a rare occurrence. Kaz had neglected to mention that his new assistant also happened to be a beauty. A *major babe,* as some of his friends would say. He was not at all pleased with the wholly unexpected flash of heat surging through him.

"Yes sir," Colleen replied. She heard the sniggers from the observers and winced. She'd snapped to attention like a new marine recruit in the presence of the camp's toughest drill instructor. She forced herself to relax her posture somewhat, managed what she hoped was a businesslike smile, and extended her hand for him to shake.

Jack took her hand in his, his grasp closing around hers. His hand was so big that it completely enveloped hers and his fingers were long and strong and hard.

Colleen tried hard not to stare, but his physical presence impacted powerfully on her senses. She had visualized Mr. Blackledge as a clone of the balding, overweight, fifty-something Kazorowski. Instead, he was the opposite—young, tall, and good-looking in a rough, purely masculine kind of way, with a shock of thick dark hair worn longish, midnight-black eyes, and a well-shaped sensual mouth now curved into a mirthless smile.

He seemed to tower over her. His frame was big and muscular and solid, in sharp contrast to her own five-feet-four, small-boned slenderness. He was wearing faded black jeans that accentuated his trim waist, flat belly, and unnerving, unmistakable virility. His black T-shirt and black leather jacket added a note of menace.

He dressed more like a thug than a newspaperman, Colleen decided nervously, and he certainly didn't look like anyone's idea of a mentor. He looked sexy and tough: the archetypical, dangerous, and hard-to-handle man whom she—the archetypical good-girl virgin—had always been careful to avoid.

"How do you do, Miss Brady," Jack said in a snidely polite tone that brought chuckles from the circle of onlookers. "I'm Jack Blackledge."

He'd planned his pseudopolite greeting, anticipating that he would have an audience, and he'd worked out a Black Jack-meets-and-quells-his-unwanted-assistant routine. He was not averse to pleasing others if it coincided with his own ends. He had not planned, however, for the unwanted assistant to be so . . . nubile. Nor had he anticipated how warm and soft and small her hand would feel in his.

Colleen gulped. "I'm pleased to meet you." Her words were reflexive. She knew she probably would have said the same thing to the devil himself. Politeness had been drilled into her, first by her mother and then by her oldest sister, Shavonne, who'd taken over the job of rearing her after their mother's death.

"Being poor is no excuse for poor manners," Mama and Shavonne had said so often that Colleen was convinced it was tatooed in her brain. The Bradys had been terribly poor at one time, and though they'd left poverty behind when four of the Brady sisters married the four wealthy Ramsey brothers, their politeness stuck. "Having money is no excuse for poor manners," was Shavonne's revised rallying cry.

"So meeting me pleases you?" Jack Blackledge's sandpaper-on-velvet voice taunted her. "Are you always so easy to please, Miss Brady?"

Colleen blushed. Someone commented on it, and she felt the hot color deepen. She silently cursed her fair coloring for revealing her just when she most wanted to appear cool and insouciant.

She withdrew her hand from his. Or tried to. Jack refused to relinquish it, giving her the unpleasant option of jerking her hand away. And that, too, would be futile, because he was stronger and he had no intention of letting go. His purpose was to rile her, unnerve her, to set up a battle for her own hand and make her look like a fool in front of her new colleagues.

Their eyes met. She read the challenge in his and was determined to meet it.

Two

"May I have my hand back?" Colleen asked with a forced, fixed smile. If she couldn't look cool and insouciant, perhaps she could sound it. She hoped no one else noticed the slight quaver in her voice.

"No." Jack grinned wickedly. He knew he had rattled her. Good. He had no intention of releasing her hand until she was so hopelessly off balance that she would go running to Kaz with a demand to be relieved of any association with that nasty Jack Blackledge.

There was another, secret, reason for his refusal to let go, one he had difficulty admitting to himself. He liked touching her.

But Colleen was not quite as naive or as easily flustered as he'd thought. After all, her four sisters had married the four Ramsey brothers, who were no slouches in the ways of aggression, intimidation, and machismo. The Brady sisters had learned how to handle the Ramsey men, no small feat, and Colleen had watched, listened, and learned a lot.

She'd seen her sisters jolly their way out of potential land-mine situations. Humor was definitely worth a try, so she put on her most dazzling smile and let her hand go limp in his. "I didn't think we'd reach the hand-holding stage so quickly, Jack. So it's love at first sight for you?"

The group laughed. Jack sensed the onlookers' approval and frowned. She was being a good sport, turning his intimidation tactics into a joke. He should drop her hand and laugh along with the gang. His frowned deepened. He didn't appreciate being outmaneuvered—especially by a baby-faced blonde.

Colleen Brady had yet to learn the ground rules, and it was time for her first lesson: He was always the one in command. Women came and went at his convenience. Everything was always on his terms; he wouldn't have it any other way. He'd even said thank you to the infuriated woman who had called him a cold-hearted snake. He'd considered it a compliment.

As it begins so shall it end. That was his motto, and he was not about to concede the opening round to little Miss Barbie Doll. His black eyes flicked over Colleen in deliberate insolent appraisal. And he found himself swallowing hard.

Her figure was enticingly curvy, hollowed and rounded in all the right places. The dark purple jersey-knit dress she wore couldn't be described as even remotely seductive, yet the soft material enhanced her every feminine attribute. She wore plain low-heeled pumps and dark stockings, modestly displaying shapely calves and slender ankles.

She had great legs, Jack conceded, wishing he could see her thighs; he was certain they were firm and rounded under that full skirt of hers. Next he tried to visualize the color and size of her nipples, and felt his body tighten with the beginnings of arousal. Scaring off little Miss Brady by seduction could turn out to be quite a pleasurable task, he decided.

"Let's make it lust at first sight, honey," he drawled. He lifted her hand to his mouth and, in the process, brought her closer. The light floral scent of her perfume wafted into his nostrils as he turned her hand over and pressed his lips against her palm.

Colleen's heart began to thud, its beat echoing in her ears. Now what should she do? She had a strong urge to snatch her hand away and smack him. But the group surrounding them was watching and waiting eagerly for her next move. One wrong move could earn her new colleagues' scorn, maybe even their enmity.

Even worse, the touch of his mouth against her sensitive palm was beginning to have a totally unsettling effect upon her. Colleen felt a peculiar heat spark in her middle and suffuse her entire body, making her face feel warm and flushed.

She glanced at his left hand. He wasn't wearing a wedding ring. The renegade thought—entirely irrelevent to her predicament—appalled her. So did these exciting, unnerving feelings his touch evoked.

"Welcome to the *T-G* and the job from hell," someone commented sardonically. "You're braver than anybody else on staff here."

"Black Jack wants an assistant just about as much as he wants a wife," somebody else muttered.

That drew an appreciative howl from the audience. It was an in joke that outsider Colleen had no trouble getting. Jack Blackledge didn't want a wife—or an assistant. Suddenly, she saw her dream job in an entirely new perspective.

"Mr. Kazorowski seemed so eager to hire me," she blurted out, too shocked by her realization to guard her tongue. "But it wasn't eagerness at all, was it? It was desperation."

There was laughter and applause. Colleen realized with a sinking sensation that she was right on target. Her plum job was a dud, one that had been rejected by countless others—probably including everyone here in the newsroom—before she'd haplessly submitted her résumé. Had Kazorowski even read the writing samples she'd submitted?

Jack abruptly dropped her hand. When her eyes

involuntarily went to his, she saw anger instead of the previous smug satisfaction.

"You also came cheap," Jack said coldly. "I hope you didn't flatter yourself into believing you were hired on the basis of your writing skill."

"I can write," Colleen insisted.

Help, she mentally implored. She didn't like to fight, and fighting with a man, especially one who was so big and dark and virile, was more than a little scary. She had watched her sisters battle their way through their initially adversarial relationships with their Ramsey husbands-to-be, and she'd felt pure relief that she was the one Brady to be spared such an ordeal.

But from observing her sisters, she'd also learned a valuable lesson: a certain breed of man, the domineering, aggressive type who brims with sexual magnetism—and Jack Blackledge definitely qualified—would run like a steamroller over anyone who meekly deferred to him. Jack Blackledge understood and respected control and strength. A docile, timid woman didn't stand a chance.

She had to prove that she could stand up to him. *Start as you mean to go on.* That was a Ramsey sentiment, meant to justify seizing control, and Colleen had observed firsthand the fate of those who ceded without a struggle. A lack of respect, no chance for self-determination. That's what would happen to her here at the *Times-Gazette* if she were to let Jack Blackledge bully her into submission.

"I can write," she reiterated more forcefully.

"You can write?" Jack mocked, his tone caustic. "You spent your summers dressed up like a duck. What's that got to do with writing? You coddled little journalism majors from your cushy academic environment—"

"I wasn't a journalism major," Colleen interrupted, her brown eyes flashing. "I majored in English."

"Even worse!" exclaimed Jack with a groan.

Colleen was dismayed. She'd tried to be a good sport and she'd tried to deflect his barbs, but Jack Blackledge meant to wear her down. She wasn't sure how long she could keep up with him.

"Aw, let her alone, Jack." One of the sportswriters, perhaps sensing her discomfiture, gave Colleen's shoulder a sympathetic pat.

"The kid's gonna be okay," the police reporter said with a chuckle.

Someone else agreed. The tide seemed to be turning in her favor. Had she passed the group's unwritten test for acceptance? When two of the younger women reporters came over and invited her to join them for lunch later, she thought maybe she had.

Jack must have thought so too. He stalked away from the group after shooting her a dark look. "Are you coming, or do you plan to hang out and goof off all day?" he called sternly. "This isn't an amusement park, you know. We have a paper to get out."

Colleen rolled her eyes heavenward. *He* was the one who'd prolonged their introduction.

"Don't let it get to you, Colleen," Susan Farley, one of her new lunch friends, murmured. "It's better that he hates you. You'll be a lot safer and last a lot longer in the job."

Colleen appreciated the words of support, but she did not feel encouraged. She followed Jack to his desk, well aware that she was not in the good graces of her new boss.

"I used to have this corner all to myself," he said sourly, "but I see they've moved in a desk for you." He pointed to the old desk crowded in between his new, larger desk and the back wall. "Sit down and get to work," he ordered.

Colleen sat down on the old wooden chair behind the desk. His chair, she couldn't help but notice, was cushioned and swiveled while this backbreaker she'd been assigned looked as if it had been discarded from a turn-of-the-century one-room schoolhouse. It felt like it, too. Sitting for long periods of time was going to be uncomfortable.

Colleen suppressed a sigh. At least the fronts of their desks were aligned so they had the lengths of both desks between them. She was thankful for small favors. Had their chairs been back-to-back, touching each other would have been unavoidable.

She remembered the size and strength and warmth of his hand gripping hers, remembered the feel of his mouth against her palm. A sensual tingle crept along her spine. Yes, she most definitely must avoid touching him.

"Do you know how to turn the computer on?" Jack asked with false solicitousness. He was watching her. "There's a little switch that you flip. Shall I help you with it?"

"No thank you, I can manage." She wouldn't accept his help, Colleen vowed, even if it meant sitting in front of a blank screen all day. She groped around the terminal until she located the switch, and the machine whirred to life.

He ignored her until she cleared her throat to say, "I hate to bother you, but exactly what am I supposed to be doing?"

"Why don't you tell me, little girl? What made you decide to play at being a newspaperwoman?"

Colleen met his gaze directly. Something intangible yet definitely forceful seemed to pass between them.

Pure sexual chemistry, Jack thought knowledgeably. Exciting but damn inconvenient under the circumstances. He was supposed to be trying to get rid of her, not take her to bed. Unfortunately, he wanted to do both.

Colleen, less experienced, interpreted the tension between them as hostility. And she'd learned from observing her sisters' hectic courtships that the only way to successfully handle hostility was to face it head-on.

She gave a silent prayer of thanks that her relationship with Jack Blackledge was strictly a professional one. Imagine having to endure a personal relationship with such a sexy, demanding, aggressive, *difficult* man! It was . . . unimaginable.

"I'm not playing at anything," she said, proud that her voice was both cool and steady. It was far easier to deal with him without the intimidating presence of an audience. "I've always wanted to write, and I could hardly believe my good luck when Mr. Kazorowski interviewed me and then told me I had the job."

"How were you to know that everybody at the *T-G* had already refused to take it?"

"Since I've met you and been subjected to your stupid little games of one-upsmanship, I can fully understand why." Colleen was pleased with her snappy comeback. Yes, it was definitely easier to fence verbally with him when the two of them were alone. It was almost . . . exciting, in an odd sort of way.

"What made you decide to apply for a job in Buffalo, of all places?" He was annoyed that her pitiful attempt to spar with him had actually stung. "I happen to love the place. I was born and raised here, but I'm well aware that our fair city doesn't enjoy a sterling national reputation. Nobody moves to Buffalo without a very specific reason."

Colleen wondered if he really wanted to know or if he was setting her up for more of his sarcasm. She chose to answer him seriously. "My roommate and I—"

"Male or female? Your roommate?" He was baiting her again.

Colleen refused even to nibble. She cast him an arch look. "Female. Her name is Nicola. Nicola Shakarian. We were best friends all through college, and after we graduated, we—"

"Have you ever lived with a man?"

"No!" She wished she hadn't sounded so shocked by the question. He'd meant to rile her again, and she'd fallen into the trap. Now she had to regain lost points. "Have you ever lived with a woman?" It was the first time she'd ever asked a man such a thing; she hoped she sounded casual and sophisticated.

"Sure. I was married for almost two years. And I've had other live-in relationships both before and since my marriage and divorce."

"Oh." *Now* what was she supposed to say? When it came to cool, casual, and sophisticated, he was light-years ahead of her.

"And before you can ask, no, I'm not living with anyone at this particular time." Jack smiled wolfishly. "I'm considered infinitely eligible."

"By whom and for what?" Colleen retorted. But she was blushing again. How had he guessed that she'd wondered about his current status?

"Touché." He actually laughed. "Is there a man in your life, Colleen? A college sweetheart who, even as we speak, is slaving away to buy you that one-quarter-carat diamond engagement ring?"

Vexedly, she shook her head no. And then her sense of humor asserted itself, and she found herself smiling. "I guess the lack of that engagement ring is one of the reasons why Nicola and I are here in Buffalo. For the first few months after graduation, we tried living in Houston. But it was impossible! My family was constantly fixing Nicola and me up with one blind date after another, and when they weren't trying to marry us off, they were dropping in and fussing over us, insisting we come over to dinner, lecturing us about safety and the perils of two single girls living alone. We decided we just had to move away. We found jobs in Washington, D.C., where lots of Nicola's relatives live."

Her smile widened. "Guess what? It was the same scene all over again, this time with *her* family driving us crazy with their overprotecting and matchmaking."

He didn't want to return her grin but found himself doing so anyway. "So you decided to seek freedom and independence in Buffalo?"

"We wanted freedom and independence anywhere! The two of us applied for jobs in cities all over the country where there weren't any Bradys or Shakarians. Nicola's a nurse and wanted to work in a pediatric hospital, and I wanted to work on a newspaper. We decided to go to the city that offered both of us the jobs we wanted."

"And it was Buffalo."

Colleen nodded. "Nicola got a job as staff nurse in the ICU at Children's Hospital. I think we're going to like it here. I know we are," she amended, her brown eyes sparkling. "We're finally completely on our own, we like our apartment, and we both have good jobs."

"Maybe your friend has a good job, but you've been suckered, kid. You've been hired to do three different jobs and paid for less than one."

She stared at him. "Three jobs?"

"In addition to working with me, which I promise will be pure torture, you'll be reviewing the nitwit teen comedies and slasher flicks when our second-banana movie reviewer goes on maternity leave. Laura Berman, our head entertainment critic, refuses to see them. And Stefanie Doebler, the food editor, has asked for somebody to take over the readers' recipe-exchange column for Thursday's expanded edition. Take a wild guess who's going to do it."

"Me?" Colleen's eyes widened.

"Bingo."

"A recipe exchange? Will I have to cook?"

"How the hell do I know?" Jack shrugged. "I've never handled a recipe-exchange column. Good Lord willing, I'll never have to."

"But I hate to cook and I'm terrible at it."

"Well, I hope you not only have to test each recipe, but you also have to eat what you've cooked. Just don't expect to pawn any of the slop off on me."

"I wouldn't dream of it." She chewed her lower lip.

"Mr. Kazorowski never mentioned that I'd be doing recipes or movie reviews."

"*Stupid* movie reviews," Jack corrected gleefully. "Of course he didn't. As you said, he was desperate. He also didn't tell you that I'm regarded as the scourge of the Buffalo newspaper world either, remember?"

Colleen regarded him thoughtfully. "You're obviously not happy that nobody wants to work with you, yet you make no attempts to be nice and friendly to—"

"Nice and friendly?" He hooted. "You worked in the magical world of Disney for too long, little girl. Nice and friendly doesn't cut it in the real world. Everyone has his own agenda and will do whatever needs to be done to promote it at the expense of anyone else. The name of the game is getting—and staying—ahead of the pack."

Colleen grimaced. "You sound a lot like my sisters' father-in-law. The father of my brothers-in-law," she added for clarification.

"Huh?" Jack clearly needed further clarification.

"I have four sisters, Shavonne, Erin, Tara, and Megan, and they're married to four brothers, Slade, Rad, Jed, and Rick. They—"

"Hey, am I supposed to remember all those names?" Jack complained. "Is there a quiz at the end of this?"

Colleen surveyed him frostily. "My sisters share the same father-in-law because their husbands have the same father. Most people find that rather interesting. And that man is something of a human shark. He would agree with you about all that doing-anything-to-anybody-to-stay-on-top junk. I don't, though," she added, her brown eyes luminous and intense.

Jack stared hard at her. This was starting to get out of hand, he realized with some alarm. She was too pretty, too shapely—and way too young for him. Furthermore, he was enjoying her company entirely too much. It was time to end the camaraderie, such as it was.

"It's not junk, it's a universal truth," he said brusquely. "And I'm not at all interested in hearing about your family, so if that's your way of being nice and friendly, don't waste it on me, *Colleen*."

Her cheeks flushed scarlet. It was bad enough that he mocked her at every turn, but now he'd even managed to turn her name into an insult. He had said *Colleen* with the same tone and inflection he would use to say *you idiot*.

She was incense. "Why are you so—so cranky?" she demanded.

"*Cranky*?" Jack snapped. "I am not *cranky*! That's a word used to describe a fractious toddler who missed his nap. Nice, Friendly, cranky. . . . If your writing vocabulary is as mundane as your speaking one, you'd better immediately invest in a good thesaurus, baby doll."

"I don't like to be referred to as baby doll or little girl," Colleen said severely. "I'm neither."

"Uh-oh, here comes the fem-lib crap. Go on, tell me how much you hate men and how we oppress all you terrifically talented women. Give me your if-women-ran-the-world-it-would-be-utopia spiel."

They glared at each other across the two desks.

"I do not hate men," Colleen said hotly. "But I might be about to make an exception in your case."

"So Colleen *likes* men." He was baiting her again, his tone silky. "And I'll bet there are lots of men who *like* Colleen. Are you a sexy little party girl with a different man every night, Colleen? Do you get your kicks out of having men chase you while you pick and choose between them?"

"No to both questions," Colleen replied stonily.

"No? You don't party, you don't tease, and you don't live in. What exactly do you do with men, Colleen?"

She didn't care for the edge in his question. Their conversation—or was it an argument?—was becoming uncomfortably similar to all those conversations she'd had with sexually hungry dates bent on bedding her. She recalled the results of all those tedious harangues.

"Are you going to tell me, Colleen?" Jack persisted. "I'm waiting with bated breath for your answer."

Colleen's lips curved into a sudden shrewd smile. She had her answer for him, all right. "Well, I could tell you that such a personal question is none of your business and even borders on sexual harassment, but I have a feeling that would only challenge you. Worse, it might incite another round of feminist bashing."

"Mmm, you're probably right," he agreed, his black eyes gleaming.

"So I'll tell you the truth." She inhaled deeply. Here goes, she thought, the declaration that sends men running—in the opposite direction. It never fails. "Sexually, I don't do much of anything with men. Maybe a good-night kiss at the door if we've gone out several times and I happen to like the person. But that's all. That's the limit of my experience with men."

"What are you saying?" Jack looked totally flummoxed. "That you're a *virgin*?"

Colleen nodded, trying valiantly to stifle the blush that was heating her whole body.

Jack gaped at her. "But—but what about sex?"

Her blush deepened, and she shifted in the uncomfortable chair. "I'm not sure if I want to have sex before I'm married or wait until afterward," she confessed softly. "My two oldest sisters, Shavonne and Erin, slept with their husbands before they were married, but my middle sister, Tara, and my youngest sister, Megan, didn't. I do know that I'd have to be deeply in love and totally committed before I'd ever make such a decision—like all my sisters were."

Jack was speechless for several moments. Finally,

he managed to splutter, "You'd actually consider *not* going to bed with a man until after he married you?"

He rose to his feet and began to pace the narrow aisle between the window and his desk. "That's medieval! It's insane, not to mention downright . . ."—he gulped for breath. "I can't even think of words strong enough to describe such an outdated, demented idea!"

"Oh, you're managing pretty well."

His reaction was not unexpected, or even original, Colleen thought with a sigh. She'd grown accustomed to similar a response every time she was pressed into confessing her reasons for "holding out," as her would-be suitors so charmingly phrased it.

"Why do men get so mad about it?" she asked, genuinely bewildered. "I don't condemn anybody who doesn't feel the same way I do about sex. I don't want to pressure anybody else into making a decision before they're ready. Why are people so quick to condemn and ridicule me?"

"Because—because—" Jack paused. Though he was loath to concede it, she did have a point. Why was he getting so upset? he wondered wildly. It wasn't as if she'd advocated enforced celibacy for him.

As if of their own volition, his eyes swept over her, taking in the sensual fullness of her lips, the vulnerable curve of her smooth, creamy neck, the rounded sweetness of her breasts under the soft jersey knit. Breasts that no man had even seen or touched.

She was a virgin! The thought seemed to boomerang throughout his brain. Why should it make him crazy that no man had ever touched her? That every intimate touch and caress would be all new for her? He firmly shut out the provocative thoughts, determined to return to the necessary business at hand— to insult her and drive her away.

"Since you're so inexperienced," he growled, "let

me clue you in on a basic fact of modern life, sweetie. Virginity is not a turn-on. If you ever hope to attract a man, don't spring your news on him."

"But that's the point. I don't want to turn you on or attract you, so I decided to tell you the truth about myself," Colleen retorted bluntly. "Now I hope you'll stop your stupid sexual innuendo. After all, it's wasted on me."

He approached her desk and stood above her, towered over her, well aware that he was trying to intimidate her. "Maybe you just made a strategical error, honey bunch. Suppose I decide to view your chastity as the ultimate challenge? Suppose I make it my goal to get you into bed? I've never failed to get any woman I want into the sack. If I should decide I want you there, baby, that's where you'll end up."

A small shiver rippled through her. It wasn't fear, Colleen realized nervously—it was excitement. Which she immediately suppressed. She already knew the outcome of this scene. "You won't bother," she said flatly. "It would take too much time and effort, and you'll quickly decide that it's not worth your while."

"Is that what happened before?"

She nodded. "But then I've never been in love before, and no one's ever been in love with me. When that happens, when I'm in love with the man who loves me—"

"You'll end up in bed without giving a thought to that gold band," Jack finished for her.

"I was going to say that he won't think I'm some stupid outdated relic. He'll respect me and let me make up my own mind without pressuring me," she countered.

"I can see why you were so comfortable in fantasyland. It's the home of unawakened beauties and noble princes and big white weddings." He shook his head. "Wake up, Colleen. Real life is not a fairy tale."

"Sometimes real life is even stranger than a fairy tale," said Colleen. "My own life—"

"Kindly spare me your life story, Colleen." His dark brows were arched, his expression sardonic.

"I wouldn't dream of inflicting it on you. Since you're so grounded in reality, you'd never believe it anyway."

"You're just full of spunk, aren't you?"

Colleen knew he was not being complimentary.

And he wasn't. All this talk about sex and love, about weddings and marriage, was getting on his nerves. It brought back unbearable memories of when he'd been a self-deluded chump who believed in happily ever after. A picture of himself at his wedding nine years ago, his bride, Donna, radiant in her white gown, flashed involuntarily across his mind.

Instantly, superimposed upon that fleeting image was another scene that had taken place less than two years after the storybook wedding. Donna, tossing clothes into a suitcase, as she icily told him she was leaving him. She'd felt cheated that the promising athlete she'd married had reneged on the deal by cutting short his baseball career. Jack, his arm in a cast from his wrist to his shoulder, his days as a highly paid major-league relief pitcher over due to a career-ending injury, had merely watched and listened.

Happily ever after. Ha! He knew better now, and he found Colleen's idealism both childish and irritating.

Jack walked back to his own desk and sat down. "Why haven't you gone running to Kaz about how mean I've been to you?" he demanded testily.

"You haven't been mean to me," Colleen assured him. "You've been—well, I hesitate to use the word again, but I will anyway—you've been cranky. I'm certainly not about to cry over that."

"I've been insulting you and tormenting you since the moment we met," Jack said through gritted teeth. "If you haven't realized that, you're either the most insensitive or the stupidest woman I've ever met."

He was desperate to make her lose control, to rage at him or burst into tears. He'd become adept at manipulating the responses of others, and he enjoyed the power it gave him. Unfortunately, Colleen Brady didn't seem to understand her role. He couldn't remember the last time he'd spent so much time and energy on someone who annoyed him this much. And met with such frustrating lack of results!

She was actually rather enjoying this, Colleen realized with some surprise. For reasons she couldn't begin to fathom, she wasn't afraid of him; paradoxically, she felt both comfortable and stimulated in his company.

"You know, it's kind of fun to thwart someone who so desperately and obviously wants to make you lose your cool," she said cheerfully. "Maybe this will make you lose *your* cool, Jack. I haven't taken personally a single thing you've said to me. All your cranky comments have rolled off me like—"

"—if you say like water off a duck's back, I won't be responsible for my actions," Jack inserted.

"Uh-oh. We'll just leave it unsaid then."

To his dismay, he almost grinned. Fortunately, he caught himself in time and restrained the urge. He was not about to succumb to her perky, spunky, feisty charm. Not him! Unfortunately, she was extremely cute and altogether too appealing. For the first time in ages, he felt off balance. He hated the feeling.

No woman was ever going to put him through *that* again, he vowed for the umpteenth time. No woman was ever going to drag him under, cause him pain, make him lose even ten minutes of sleep at night. Not ever again.

He stood up. "I sometimes work at home, but Kaz insisted that I meet you here today. Okay, I've met you. Now I'm leaving. If you want to do something constructive with your time, you can read up on who's who and what's happening in Buffalo or you can read the backlist of my columns or else go to the movie critic and the food editor and introduce yourself. I don't particularly care what you do. I'm outta here."

Grabbing his beat-up attaché case, he stalked from the newsroom. It wasn't a defensive move, he assured himself. He was not escaping from Colleen Brady. Jack Blackledge didn't run from smart, sexy little virgins, even if they did refuse to be cowed by him. He was going home because he felt like it, and he always did what he felt like doing.

He repeated those words like a mantra the whole way home.

Three

Colleen arrived back at her apartment that after-noon shortly before four with a handful of recipes, a bound edition of the complete collection of col-umns by Black Jack, and a thick legal pad filled with notes. Nicola, who'd worked the seven-to-three-thirty shift at Children's Hospital, was already home.

"Throw on a pair of jeans and a sweater, Colleen." Nicola was already wearing exactly that. "We've got dates tonight."

"Dates?" echoed Colleen without enthusiasm.

"Mine's a pediatric surgical resident. You know, a resident is a doctor who's taking specialized train-ing and it takes at least five years to be a board-certified pediatric surgeon. Your date is his friend."

Colleen sighed, frowning. "Another blind date. I left Houston and Washington to escape those, remember?"

"This is different," Nicola said cheerfully. "We're supposed to meet the guys at about six at this pizza place one block down from the hospital."

"Your first day on the job and you've already met someone to go out with. You're amazing, Nic. But do you really need me to go along for the friend?" Colleen sighed again. "I have a lot of reading to do, and I'm so tired I feel like going straight to bed and not waking up till next week."

"That doesn't sound like you, Colleen. Why so exhausted? Didn't it go well today? What's Mr. Blackledge like?"

"Not at all what I expected," Colleen said wryly. Nor had she expected the peculiar flatness that had gripped her after he'd left the newsroom. It had grown worse during lunch, when she'd been regaled with the list of Black Jack's conquests. She'd left work dispirited.

"What does that mean? Is he better, worse, what?" demanded Nicola.

"I don't want to talk about Jack Blackledge. I'm too tired and he's too exhausting a subject." Not to mention confusing—distancing and sarcastic, but with an undercurrent of . . . something else. She didn't want to think about him anymore, either.

Colleen went to her room to change, and Nicola traipsed along after her. "Tell me about this pediatric surgical resident of yours, Nic."

Nicola ran her hand through her long, raven-black hair. She and Colleen were the same height and weight, but Nicola's dark hair and olive complexion contrasted sharply with Colleen's fair coloring. Though they both had brown eyes, they joked that Colleen's were the color of milk chocolate while Nicola's were like the bittersweet variety.

"I met him in the intensive care unit this morning. I'm taking care of two of his patients there," Nicola said, flopping back on the bed with a happy sigh. "We hit it off immediately, and he asked me to have lunch with him in the cafeteria. We did, and then he asked me to have dinner with him at the pizza place near the hospital. He's on call tonight," she added.

"What about my date?" Colleen asked resignedly.

"He's an intern at Children's, from Pakistan or . . . I'm not exactly sure where. He doesn't speak much English, but he can read it well and—"

"My date doesn't speak English? Nicola, how am I supposed to communicate with him? I can't spend the evening writing him notes."

"Oh, don't worry about it, Colleen," Nicola said breezily. "You'll be fine. After all, Kamal and I will be there too."

"Kamal?"

"My date, Kamal Veli. He's a hunk, Colleen. Dark hair, dark eyes, swarthy complexion. He's so smart and dedicated, and he has the most wonderful way with the children. Oh, Colleen, it's just amazing! He and I share so many of the same tastes in music and books and movies!"

"Obviously *he* speaks and understands English," Colleen said dryly. She paused. "Nicola, remember the last time you dated someone named Kamal? I certainly do. It was while we were living in Washington. Your family went beserk because he was of Turkish descent and you're of Armenian descent and Turks are the Armenians' worst enemy in the world. I've never been too strong in history, but I know all about Turkey and Armenia's blood feud from listening to your hysterical relatives while you were going out with Kamal."

"That was Kemal, spelled with an *e*," Nicola corrected, pronouncing the name slightly differently. "Kamal's not Turkish, he's from the Soviet Union." She averted her eyes from Colleen's. "More precisely, from the Soviet republic of Azerbaijan."

"I know that place too! I've heard your family talk about it!" Colleen stared at her. "Azerbaijan and Armenia are currently embroiled in a conflict. Nicola, remember the emergency relief supplies your family was collecting last year to send over—"

"Of course I remember," Nicola interrupted. "But what's that got to do with Kamal and me? I've never been near Armenia in my life, and he came to the States fifteen years ago to live with his aunt and uncle. He went to college and med school here in

Buffalo, and he intends to become an American citizen."

"You don't have to defend yourself to me, Nic," Colleen said soothingly. "I think ethnic and religious differences are irrelevant here in America, but your family went nuts when you dated Kemal, and they'll probably have the same reaction to Kamal."

Nicola laughed, her dark eyes sparkling with excitement. "Colleen, we're in Buffalo to escape our interfering families, remember?"

The telephone kept ringing. Jack, deeply involved in honing the final paragraph of his column, planned to ignore it. After all, the caller was bound to give up sooner or later.

Unfortunately for him, the persistent caller had decided on later. The monotonous rings continued. Jack's train of thought had been totally derailed.

"Yeah?' he barked into the phone.

There was a moment's pause. And then a female's voice, cool and well-modulated: "Jack Blackledge? This is Ariel Morgan. My aunt Polly is a friend and customer of your mother and your aunts' gift shop in Florida."

It took extraordinary restraint for Jack to keep from howling in protest and slamming down the receiver. He knew what Ariel Morgan was going to say before she uttered the words. Jack silently mouthed the all-too-familiar sentence as Ariel spoke it.

"When they realized that we were in the same city, they insisted that I give you a call."

His mother and her two sisters, all widows who jointly owned and operated a card, gift, and doll shop in Orlando, were forever running across relatives of women they deemed suitable matrimonial prospects for him. His phone number was passed along, and he invariably received calls from hopeful would-be mates. Not one of whom had ever been right for him.

"I teach English literature at the University of Buffalo and am also involved with their poetry workshop," the woman continued as Jack silently groaned.

Yes, Aunt Dorothy, Aunt Judy, and Mom had done it again. A professor of literature who dabbled in poetry was hopelessly removed from a three-columns-a-week newspaperman.

"Since we're both writers, our well-meaning relatives thought we should meet." There was condescending amusement in Ariel Morgan's tone.

As if she were calling simply to humor the old dears, Jack thought snidely. She wasn't, he knew. She'd called because it fit her own purposes. As he'd told Colleen, everybody had an agenda.

"I've read your column," Ariel continued. "You do show a . . . certain style that, with effort and assistance, could be reworked into the format of a novel."

Here it comes. Jack grimaced. The when-are-you-going-to-stop-writing-for-newspapers-with-their-prole-readership-and-join-the-intelligentsia-by-writing-a-work-of-Important-Fiction spiel. He'd heard it before from Ariel Morgan clones. He yawned as she spouted her own version of it.

He supposed he must be as prole as his readership, for he had no desire to take on the Great American Novel—or any other kind of Serious Fiction. And though he knew his mother and aunts meant well, he had no desire to take on Ariel Morgan, either.

When she suggested meeting for dinner later this week, he begged off. She was persistent—those seventeen rings on the phone should have clued him in to that—and suggested the following week, then the next. Jack shook his head. He was going to have to convince her that he was busy for the rest of his life. And do it tactfully. If only his mother and aunts weren't involved! Black Jack had one soft spot in his hardened heart and it was for those three ladies.

"Listen, Arlene—"

"Ariel," she corrected. "The name of the spirit in Shakespeare's *Tempest*, the sylph in Pope's *Rape of the Lock*. Truly, I was born to teach English lit."

Just as he'd been born to play baseball, mused Jack. And when that dream had died, he'd landed in the newspaper world, far from Ariel Morgan's land of literature. "Ariel, I didn't want to get personal, but the truth is . . . , uh, I'm dating someone steadily right now. It's pretty serious and we've decided—" he cleared his throat. This was not an excuse he'd used before. How would one phrase it? "We've decided not to see anyone else. Sort of an exclusivity contract, if you will."

He must have pulled it off. Ariel Morgan believed him. She sounded disconcerted, then annoyed, and quickly hung up.

Pleased with his ingenuity, Jack returned to his column, taking time to remove the receiver from its cradle. There would be no more unwanted phone calls for the remainder of the evening.

He remembered to replace the receiver before he went to bed, shortly after midnight. Almost instantaneously, the phone began to ring.

"Jack, I've been trying to reach you for hours." His mother's voice, definitely accusatory, came across the wire. "You took the phone off the hook again, didn't you?"

"Sure did, Mom." He was cheerfully unapologetic. If there was something wrong, his mother wouldn't take time to berate him before launching into details. "What's up?"

"You tell me. Polly Morgan called earlier to tell me that her niece had called you and that you told her you were seriously involved with someone."

"Ariel Morgan called her aunt to tell her that?" Jack exclaimed incredulously. "Why would she do such a thing?" Damn, he'd thought she had bought his excuse. Obviously she hadn't, and had decided to retaliate by dragging their relatives into the fray.

"She was a bit put out that her aunt had given her the name and number of a man who was already spoken for. Polly called here to find out what's going on. What *is* going on, Jack?" His mother didn't bother to suppress the rising excitement in her voice. "Who is she, this girl you're serious about? Aunt Dorothy and Aunt Judy and I are so excited. We want to know all about her."

Oh, what a tangled web we weave when first we practice to deceive. Jack remembered the collection of needlepoint pillows that his mother kept on a loveseat in her bedroom. That ominous warning had been neatly stitched onto one of them. He should have heeded its message, Jack thought as he searched for a description of his imaginary love.

Unfortunately, fiction wasn't his strong suit. "She—well—she's pretty indescribable, Mom." *Lame, Blackledge,* he admonished himself, but it was the best he could do without advance warning. "I know you and Aunt Dorothy and Aunt Judy would like her," he added, straining for credibility.

To his relief, his mother seemed content with that. "Oh Jack, I'm so happy and so *relieved* that you've found someone at last. I know how badly hurt you were when Donna—"

"Let's not get into ancient history," Jack interrupted tightly. "Anyway, divorcing Donna wasn't that big a deal. It was bound to happen sooner or later and—"

"You're right, son, what's past is past." It was his mother's turn to interrupt. "Tomorrow I'm booking a flight to Buffalo for Judy, Dorothy, and me. With scheduling luck, we'll be in town the day after. Your cousins can mind the store while we're gone."

"What?"

"We've been planning to visit you anyway," his mother continued blithely. "We've gotten so spoiled since you've taken to visiting us down here that we haven't been back to Buffalo in over four years. Now it's definitely our turn to travel. Don't worry. We won't move in with you, we'll stay at a hotel. And of course we want to meet and spend time with you and your new love."

His new love? Jack was aghast. He couldn't talk her out of the spontaneous visit, though he certainly tried. By the time Jack hung up the phone, his mother and aunts were counting the hours until they saw him again—and met his new true love.

Who didn't exist.

Jack's mood was very black as he gazed at the ceiling and contemplated his fate.

Jack was already at his desk when Colleen arrived at the newsroom the next morning. He watched her walk toward her desk, his eyes lingering on her bright face, then lowering to her curvy figure.

She was wearing a fitted black knit jumper and a black-and-white striped shirt, black stockings, and flat black shoes, her hair pulled into a high ponytail that swung perkily as she walked. The hemline o the jumper was short, a few inches above her knee and once again he admired the shapeliness of he legs. Her breasts were firm and high, her waist intriguingly small, her hips nicely flared. She was subtly sexy, managing to look alluring as well as young and fresh and innocent all at the same time.

And all of which she was, of course. Exactly the type of wholesome, all-American girl he had assidu-ously avoided, even when *he* was young and whole-some. Back then, he'd been eager to lose his innocence and had divined early on that it was the flashy, trashy bad girls who could make that hap-pen. As the years passed, he saw no reason to alter his preferences.

Other men might look for character and depth, intelligence and compassion in the women they dated, but Jack wanted cheap thrills. His family was forever warning him that if he didn't settle down soon with a woman of quality, "all the good ones will be taken and you'll end up alone—or be forced to settle for someone nobody else wanted."

Jack didn't consider those well-intentioned warnings a dire threat; he found them hilarious.

He knew there were those who might say he'd gotten exactly what he deserved when sultry, shallow Donna walked out on him with a casual shrug. But his mother and aunts had refrained from uttering a single "I told you so" about Donna. He appreciated that, because they *had* told him so, long before he'd ever married her.

Jack watched Colleen smile her way through the newsroom, greeting her coworkers. Nice and friendly. He had ridiculed her for it, but Colleen was the epitome of the girl a dutiful son takes home to Mother. If he introduced *her* to his mother and aunts, they would be delighted and reassured of his happiness and well-being. They would also return to Florida more quickly and stop their infernal matchmaking.

It was the perfect plan, and he'd been perfecting the details since he'd hatched it last night. There was only one hitch: gaining Colleen's cooperation. A trifling obstacle, Jack decided. Sweet little Miss Brady was no match for Black Jack's notorious charm.

"Hi." Colleen was breathless when she reached her desk—because she'd rushed from her car through the newsroom, she assured herself. Certainly, her heartbeat hadn't gone into double time because she'd seen Jack Blackledge sprawled sexily in his chair as she'd crossed the city room. Today his jeans were a well-worn blue and his shirt was navy, but the change in color didn't alter his aura of sexual danger. She tensed.

Jack turned on the full force of the Blackledge smile. "Good morning, Colleen."

Colleen carefully hung her purse over the back of

her chair, laid her plastic carry-all on her desk and slowly unzipped it.

"That's a handy-looking case you've got there," Jack said brightly. "Canary-yellow, hm? Makes a nice splash of color."

Colleen stared at him, waiting. His smile widened, and her brows narrowed. "Go on. Say it," she said at last.

"Say what?"

"Whatever wisecrack you're going to make about this case."

"I just told you how much I like it, Colleen."

"You don't expect me to believe you, do you?"

"Why shouldn't you? Say, can I get you a cup of coffee or a soda from the machine?"

"No thank you, I brought my own coffee today." She removed a kelly-green mug and a matching thermos from the case.

Jack watched her unscrew the cap of the thermos and pour hot coffee into the mug. "I bet you make great coffee," he enthused. "May I try a cup?" He pulled his own mug with a Buffalo Bills logo on it from a desk drawer and walked over to her desk. He was still smiling.

Colleen's hand trembled a little as she filled the mug.

He took a long swallow. "Ah, just as I thought. You make extraordinary coffee, Colleen." He smiled down at her.

Colleen took several steps backward. "Why are you doing this?" she asked warily.

He appeared genuinely astonished. "I don't know what you mean."

"You keep *smiling* at me. It's . . . It's creepy." The tip of her tongue glided over her lips, moistening them.

"My smile is creepy?" Jack was taken aback. And insulted. For years he'd been complimented on the irresistibility of his smile; he'd come to believe wholeheartedly in its potency. *And she'd called it creepy?*

"I have a fairly good idea of what you're trying to do, you know," she said.

"Oh, do you?"

She nodded. "You're deliberately being inconsistent. Yesterday you were sarcastic and snappish, so I came to work today expecting more of the same. Instead, you flash that big smile, which is as phony as a counterfeit bill, and act friendly. So next time I'll be expecting that, but you'll do something different. I learned in Psych 101 that people and animals can adjust to most anything but inconsistency. You don't want me to adjust to you. You're trying to goad me into telling Mr. Kazorowski that we can't work together."

"Clever little Colleen," Jack growled. "You think you've got it all figured out, don't you?" He was annoyed that she'd seen through him so swiftly. She'd mistaken his motives but not his insincere charm.

"I'm right, aren't I?"

He gave a short laugh, but he was not amused. "I must be slipping. My phony smile and charm used to be foolproof."

"Only against fools." Colleen sat down on her hard wooden chair. Jack watched her delve into the case and bring out a number of letters and newspaper clippings.

"What's all that?" he asked, curious despite himself.

"The last two months' worth of the readers' recipe-exchange column and the letters and recipes that the readers sent in." She picked up a letter. "Someone writes in and asks for a certain recipe, like this one: 'My grandmother used to make a dense, moist chocolate cake with oil in it. I know she used cocoa powder from a tin. Does anyone have this recipe?' Then I sort through the readers' responses and find a recipe for a dense, moist chocolate cake with oil and cocoa powder in it."

Jack grimaced. "That's not journalism, that's cooking."

"Stefanie Doebler says I don't have to try out the recipes myself, though. Thank heavens for that! But some are pretty interesting. Listen to this one, named Dessert Spectacular—it has fruit cocktail, marshmallows, whipped cream, two different kinds of pudding, and three different kinds of Jell-O, all layered in a deep dish."

"It sounds disgusting. You should retitle it Dessert Emetic."

Colleen shot him a reproving glance. "It's from a lady who lives in the township of Tonawanda, wherever that is. I'm going to use it in Thursday's column, along with two dense-chocolate cake recipes and two requests for new recipes."

She turned on her terminal and began to type. Jack fidgeted. Things were not going as he'd planned. She was supposed to have succumbed to his irresistible charm so he could suggest a quiet lunch, where he would make his outrageous request; to pretend to be "seriously involved" with him during his mother and aunts' visit. Last night he'd been sure that he could charm her into agreeing. Now, for the first time, he had the uneasy feeling that she might not be quite so pliant.

Well, if at first you don't succeed . . . He didn't get where he was today by giving up after the first try. He hitched his leg on the corner of her desk so that he was half sitting on the edge. If friendly didn't work, there was always the sympathy angle, one he'd successfully used before. But he must be subtle, lead into it carefully . . .

"My latest syndicated column ran in the paper yesterday afternoon and will be carried in the morning dailies today," he said conversationally. "Did you read it?"

Colleen's eyes strayed to the hard-muscled length

of his leg, resting less than a foot away from her. Her pulse began to beat a little faster, and she caught her lower lip between her teeth.

"Yes," she said, quickly looking away. "It was entertaining. Informative, too. I haven't been following the disagreement between the NFL players' union and the team owners, but you brought me up to date. Do you think the football players will strike, or were you playing devil's advocate in the column?"

"Unfortunately, I think there will be a football strike by the end of the month." Jack's dark eyes glowed as he outlined the whys and wherefores. His enthusiasm for his subject was infectious.

"I like the way you didn't take sides in your column," Colleen said admiringly. "You said everybody involved is equally greedy, but you weren't preachy about it, you were funny."

"How did you like that quote I used—'What's mine is mine; what's yours is negotiable'? I've found it's applicable to a wide range of greedy souls, from professional athletes and celebrities to the common garden variety of ex-wife. Mine included."

Colleen shifted in her chair. Discussing an ex-wife was something she'd never done with a man. Her dates were invariably in her own age group, men who had yet to marry let alone divorce. Then she reminded herself that Jack Blackledge was her boss, not a potential date. Her cheeks pinked slightly. "I see," she said neutrally.

Ah, she'd snapped at the bait he'd so cleverly dangled. Jack congratulated himself. "Yeah, Donna had a severe case of gimme-it-all." He shrugged artfully. "When I married her nine years ago, I was riding pretty high—big pro baseball contract, endorsements. I was even a pretty hot baseball card. When we split up, Donna wanted everything."

"Did she get it?" Colleen held her breath, hoping she didn't sound like a curious snoop. But she was too intrigued by his personal life to resist asking the question.

"The court saw fit to award her her freedom and nothing else," Jack replied evenly. "There were a number of circumstances working in my favor. We'd been married less than two years, we had no children, and I'd supported her since the day of our wedding. Of course, there wasn't a whole lot left of my baseball earnings, either—Donna liked to live the good life, so to speak. While we were married, we lived it, all at my expense. Oh yes, I also contested her suit with one of my own, on the grounds of adultery. I was granted the divorce," he added as a throwaway.

Colleen sat, silent and motionless, again unsure of how to respond. Divorcing his unfaithful wife—who'd spent all his money!—must have been painful, yet Jack appeared unaffected by it all. She wondered whether he'd adjusted and put it all behind him or he was suppressing a maelstrom of emotion. She wasn't sure, and he offered no clues.

"It must have been a very difficult time for you," she said at last, choosing her words carefully. He was confiding in her and she was both flattered and deeply interested. Yet wary. Her instincts, usually quite reliable, warned her that something was not quite right.

Jack shrugged. "Losing the chance to play baseball was a thousand times worse than shedding Donna." His eyes met Colleen's and he was surprised at what he saw there. Sympathy, yes, but also suspicion.

Frowning, he leaned closer. A faint whiff of her perfume drifted toward him. He remembered the scent, remembered its distracting sensual allure. For one dizzying moment, his head clouded and his mind went blank. He fought a perverse urge to touch the alabaster smoothness of her cheek.

He was very, very near. Colleen inhaled a shuddering breath. Her heart was racing and her insides felt like warm honey. "How did you lose the chance to play baseball?" she heard herself ask in a soft, throaty voice she hardly recognized as her own.

Her question jolted Jack from his sensual reverie. He had a game plan to follow, he reminded himself. If he expected to win—and he did—he'd better proceed accordingly.

"I was in a car accident and my arm was crushed," he said, leaning a bit closer. And then he succumbed to the irresistible impulse to touch her bouncy ponytail. It felt as soft and silky as it looked. He took a strand of her hair between his two fingers and rubbed sensuously.

"There were two breaks in my arm that were compound fractures and they did some permanent nerve damage," he continued huskily. "The doctors told me I would regain the use of my arm, but I'd never be able to pitch again. They were right, and accepting *that* decree was far more traumatic than being handed my divorce decree."

Feeling his fingers glide through her hair sent shivers of awareness through her. Colleen stood up and moved from her chair. He was entirely too close for comfort, and she had the uneasy feeling that he'd planned it that way. But why?

"Where are you going?" Jack said raspily. He knew he shouldn't have touched her. What was thoroughly disconcerting was that he'd been unable to stop himself from doing so. For a few brief moments Jack Blackledge had lost control.

"I'm going to stand here." Colleen stood at the far end of her desk, her arms folded in front of her chest. She looked both defensive and vulnerable.

"Why? All I was doing was talking to you, Colleen." He was wrong and they both knew it, but he wasn't about to admit to anything more.

"You were leaning over me, you were *hovering* over me," she countered. "You were—" She paused to swallow, hard. "You were playing with my hair. And why were you telling me those things about yourself? Yesterday you told me to spare you my life story, but today you're sharing part of yours. What are you up to, Jack?"

Jack felt a surge of color sweep from his neck to his face. This was ridiculous, not to mention embarrassing. He wasn't accustomed to being grilled by a woman he'd been attempting to charm. "Maybe I decided to follow your advice and be nice and friendly," he growled.

"I don't believe you," Colleen said flatly. "I think you were trying to make me feel sorry for you. What I don't understand is why."

Jack heaved a sigh. "You know, you're not as gullible as I'd counted on, kid. You're right. I was trying to play on your sympathy."

Astonished by his admission, she walked back toward him. "But why?" she asked, wide-eyed.

"Because I wanted you to do me a favor." To his perturbation, she began to laugh. "What's so funny?" he demanded.

"You are. Why didn't you come right out and ask me?"

"Because it's one of the stupidest favors I've ever had to ask for, and I thought I'd have a better shot at your compliance if your soft little heart was bleeding for me."

"Just ask me, Jack. After all, you're my boss. I'd have to be crazy to turn down the chance to do you a favor, right?"

Jack grimaced. "Keeping that in mind, would you like to have dinner with me tomorrow night?"

Her heart lurched crazily. He was asking her out. The elation that surged through her was thrilling as well as enlightening; she hadn't realized just how much she wanted to go out with him.

"Don't worry, it's not a real date," Jack hastened to assure her. "I'm well aware that you and I are total opposites, that we have nothing in common and no desire to—uh—further our relationship outside the office."

Colleen felt like a helium-filled balloon that had

just been pricked. She was abruptly, shockingly deflated. She schooled her features into what she hoped was a semblance of indifference. "You're absolutely right," she said. He *was*, she insisted to herself. She must have been suffering from a temporary lapse of sanity to think otherwise. "So why do you want me to have dinner with you?"

"Because you're not the only one with well-meaning, meddlesome relatives. My mother and her two sisters would like nothing better than to see me settled down with a nice girl. Even though they're in Florida, they still manage to send a slew of prospects my way. Trouble is, their idea of a nice girl isn't mine."

"That I can imagine." It was rather funny, picturing cool Jack at the mercy of his matchmaking mama and aunts. It humanized him a bit.

"To make a long story short, I made the mistake of telling them that I was involved with a nice, suitable girl. My mother and aunts are arriving in Buffalo tomorrow to visit me and meet this paragon. That's where you come in, Colleen. Will you play the part? You'll be making three sixty-something widows very happy, not to mention gaining points with your boss."

"But you must know lots of women you could ask besides me," Colleen protested.

He shook his head. "The women I usually date are not meet-the-family material. That's why I date them. I don't want to get involved, I don't want them to meet my family, and I don't want to meet theirs. Say you'll do it, Colleen," he coaxed.

"I don't think it's right, deceiving your family like that. What's the point?"

"The point is they'll return to Florida content that I've given up my wicked ways and thinking I have been reformed by the love of a good woman. And they'll stop handing out my phone number to every unattached woman's mother, aunt, or grandma who comes into their gift shop."

"And afterward, if they start asking about our future plans—and you know they will—what will you tell them?"

"I'll say that we're still dating but haven't set the big date yet. I can use that one for years. Meanwhile, I'll be free from all those maternal warnings and aunty advice, free from their matchmaking attempts and the intolerable blind dates that go with it! And on the flip side, my mother and aunts can stop worrying about me and can concentrate their energies on their shop and on my cousins and their families."

"I don't know, Jack."

"You could benefit too, Colleen," he said quickly. "If you ever need me to play the part of suitable suitor when *your* relatives come to Buffalo, you've got it, babe."

Colleen regarded him thoughtfully. He believed that people operated according to their own self-serving agendas, and he was appealing to hers. What if her family were to start in the long-distance matchmaking game? If Jack's mother and aunts could drive him to distraction with their attempts, imagine what the high-powered Ramseys could do if they began to send eligible swains to Buffalo for her?

"I can't believe this, but I'm starting to consider it," she admitted. "I don't have anything to do tomorrow night, and if I'm out with you, Nicola can't drag me along on any more blind dates. Last night was the worst!"

"You had a date last night?" he asked quickly, too quickly. He frowned.

Colleen didn't notice his timing or his frown. She was recalling last night's debacle. "My date hadn't slept for the past thirty-one hours—he's an intern and had been on call—and his English isn't good even when he's fully alert. He didn't say a single word all evening, not one. He just sort of stared at the pizza with glazed eyes and finally fell sound asleep, with his face right on the table. Of course, Nicola and Kamal were too absorbed in each other to even notice. They sat by themselves in a booth across the restaurant for three solid hours, until Kamal got paged. I was dying of boredom. I did the crossword puzzle on the placemat over and over."

"You won't have any evenings like that with me, I promise." Jack smiled purposefully. "My mother and my aunts and I all speak English, and we don't fall asleep in restaurants. Say yes, Colleen."

She tilted her head. "Well, okay," she said at last. "There's nothing worth watching on TV tomorrow night anyway."

"How flattering," Jack said dryly. "I hope you'll show a little more enthusiasm for my company when we're with my mother and my aunts."

"Exactly how enthusiastic am I supposed to be?"

"Just act as if you're in love with me, and I'll do the same."

"That should be easy for you—you are in love with yourself."

He raised his dark brows. "I trust you won't make remarks like that in front of them. You're supposed to be my sweet, adoring girlfriend."

"I'd better enroll in an acting class."

They smiled at each other, tentatively at first, then with genuine warmth and humor. "So do we have a deal?" Jack asked, extending his hand.

"We have a deal." Colleen put her hand in his.

Four

"We're supposed to meet them at the View from the Top Restaurant in Niagara Falls," Jack said grimly the moment Colleen opened her apartment door. "Yeah, it's as corny as its name implies. You have to understand that my mother and aunts are incorrigible romantics. They probably think that viewing the Falls some twenty stories up, while dining and dancing, will inspire me to propose to you right on the spot."

"Should I accept?" Colleen asked with a teasing grin.

"Not unless you want to be married to me. I wouldn't put it past that trio to have a marriage license and a justice of the peace on hand just in case I happened to *pop the question*."

Colleen laughed. "They're that desperate to marry you off?"

"I have no sisters or brothers, and my mother is desperate for grandchildren. Her sisters both have them and she feels deprived."

"Will she ever get them?" Colleen asked curiously. "Grandchildren, I mean."

"She may, eventually," Jack shrugged. "I like kids. If I find a woman with enough money to make marriage worth my while, I'll marry her and have them."

"Enough money to make marriage worth your while?" Colleen echoed incredulously.

"I'm not greedy—a million or two will do." He smiled a shark's smile. "Naturally, there will be no prenuptial agreement."

"What's yours is yours and what's hers is negotiable?"

"You catch on quick, kid. Too bad you're not rich, hm? You might've had a chance with me."

"I think I've had a lucky escape," Colleen retorted coolly.

She didn't feel as cool as she sounded. In the few days she'd known Jack Blackledge, there had never been a reason for her to mention that the four brothers her sisters had married were scions of the wealthy Ramsey family, owners of a mall-development-and-management empire that had created 130 state-of-the-art shopping malls in thirty-two states. It was hardly a fact one casually dropped into a conversation, especially since Jack had made it clear that he didn't care to hear about her family.

And now that he'd revealed his unscrupulous marriage plans, it definitely wouldn't be prudent to mention that the late Augusta Ramsey, who'd lived next door to the Bradys in West Virginia, had generously provided for the orphaned sisters in her will. Colleen's inheritance from old Augusta Ramsey had grown to nearly $5 million, thanks to wise investing and managing by her Ramsey in-laws.

But being hand-to-mouth poor for the first sixteen years of her life had left its mark. Colleen could never quite shake the feeling that her newfound financial security could disappear as quickly and unexpectedly as it had appeared. No amount of reassurances from her sisters or the Ramseys could convince her otherwise. She'd studied hard in preparation for a career and had worked throughout her college years, never permitting herself the luxury of depending on her inheritance. The interest from her trust fund provided supplemental income to her earnings, but Colleen used it sparingly.

She had listened to the Ramseys rail about fortune hunters; she'd heard them congratulate themselves on never having succumbed to the wiles of the money hungry. But until this moment, Colleen had never given a thought to the possibility of being a target herself. To be deliberately and cold-bloodedly married for her bank account . . . a chill coursed through her.

It wouldn't happen to her, Colleen promised herself. Maybe she'd been naive not to realize the risk before, but Jack Blackledge had unwittingly clued her in on the danger. Yes, she'd had a very lucky escape.

"You look like an antifur activist staring into the window of a furrier's salon," Jack teased. "I take it you don't approve of my mercenary marital plans."

Her disapproval clearly amused him, heightening her indignation. "I certainly don't. You know how it feels to be used for your money—your wife did that to you—and I can't understand how you could ever consider hurting anybody else that way."

His smile faded. "You're supposed to be playing the part of my girlfriend, not my spiritual adviser, so please skip the sermonizing. And for your reference, my former wife didn't marry me for money." Jack grimaced. "She married me for my pitching talent and an entry into the world of major-league baseball. When it was gone, so was she."

"And so was your money," Colleen added succinctly, though Jack looked ready to throttle her. She wasn't about to let him weasel out of acknowledging the truth.

A heavy silence fell over the room; the tension between them was almost palpable. Colleen was inordinately grateful when Nicola, wrapped in a full-length terry-cloth robe, a towel covering her wet hair turban-style, rushed into the living room.

"Colleen, did I get any calls while I was in the shower?" Nicola asked urgently.

"Kamal called," replied Colleen. "He said he'll pick you up in an hour."

"An hour!" shrieked Nicola. "I'll never be ready!" She bolted from the room.

"That was Nicola," Colleen said, grinning. "I'd've introduced you, but—"

"I understand. Time is crucial when Kamal is due within the hour. Uh, who's Kamal?"

"He's a pediatric surgical resident at Children's Hospital who's about to become Buffalo's entry in the Armenian-Azerbaijani feud."

"What?"

She explained about the Shakarians' loyalty to their motherland, about Nicola's rebellious fling with the Turkish Kemal and this new, fledgling relationship with Kamal Veli.

"Families!" Jack threw up his hands. "You can't live without them, but living with them is definitely easier if they're hundreds of miles away."

"And even then, they make their presence felt," Colleen put in. "This dinner of ours tonight is a case in point."

They faced each other.

"Do I need a coat?" Colleen asked, purposefully redirecting the conversation. Money, marriage, and family held too many risks. "It was fairly warm this afternoon, but with the sun down and the wind blowing—"

"It's great, invigorating. Skip the coat."

His eyes flicked over her. She was dressed in the type of tasteful, stylish outfit a young woman might wear to meet her steady beau's family for the first time: a silk cream-colored two-piece dress with bright blue polka dots that had a demure neckline, elbow-length sleeves, and a short, swingy skirt.

His mother and aunts would not consider her attire gut-wrenchingly sexy; it was his own prurient imagination that caused him to view her in such a way. He couldn't seem to stop himself from focusing on the shapeliness of her legs, encased in sheer cream-colored stockings and bright blue high-heeled shoes. He found himself wondering what she was wearing under her dress and felt himself begin to grow warm.

Did she have a predilection for the type of racy lingerie sold through catalogs that featured pictures as steamy as yesterday's centerfolds? Or did she prefer old-fashioned lace and ribbons, which, in their own way, could be as enticing and sexy as the X-rated stuff. His mouth grew dry.

This would never do. Jack reminded himself that he was enduring an evening with this hopelessly antiquated little puritan in order to dupe his mother and aunts. Speculating on the virginal Miss Brady's underwear was an exercise in futility—she undoubtedly wore thick opaque cotton that primly contained and concealed everything.

He tugged irritably at the collar of his starched white shirt, then attacked the knot of his tie, loosening it. "I hate getting all duded up like this," he growled. He pulled on the arms of his suit coat and gave his shoulders a violent shrug, as if trying to repel the hapless jacket.

"You remind me of my little nephews, Connor and Christopher, in their Sunday suits." Colleen smiled at the thought of them. "They loathe being duded up too."

But his semblance to the truculent small boys ended there. There was not a thing little-boyish about Jack Blackledge, she thought, her pulse quickening. This was the first time she'd seen him in a suit, and he looked wonderfully distinguished, exuding an aura of raw power. He projected sexual magnetism no matter what he was wearing. Colleen felt a rush of unwelcome excitement surge through her.

She reminded herself that this *fortune hunter* ought to induce nausea, not a thundering heartbeat. She would get through this evening because she'd promised to do so; she would be pleasant and polite but impersonal. And she would never, ever make the mistake of going out with him again. Not for any reason.

Jack took another swipe at his tie, and Colleen flashed a saccharine smile. "I'm sure your mother and aunts will appreciate your wearing a suit, especially if they know what a sacrifice it is for you."

Jack's scowl deepened. She had a small dimple in her left cheek when she smiled. Oh, she was entirely too alluring. Her mouth was too temptingly soft, her big brown eyes expressive. They captivated him with their range, bright and alert, gleaming with humor, darkening with anger. He wondered how those velvety eyes would look when lit with passion or drowsy with sensual satiation.

His body begin to tighten and throb with an ache that was rampantly sexual. He reminded himself that she was an entire decade younger than himself, that when he'd married Donna, Colleen Brady had been in junior high school.

His dark gaze lingered compulsively on the soft, feminine lines of her body. The trouble with that defense was that she looked nothing like a junior high school student tonight. Because she wasn't one. She was very much an adult, an irresistible, desirable woman. And a dangerous one, because she played by a whole different set of rules than he did. Jack was suddenly, intensely furious with her. It was imperative to establish the requisite antipathy between them.

"I own one suit, this one. I wear it mainly to funerals. I suppose it's apropos that I'm wearing it tonight," he added darkly.

"You see similarities between going out to dinner with me and attending a funeral?" He didn't sound as if he was kidding. "Well, keep in mind that I'm only doing this as a *favor* to you," Colleen said tartly. She gave her hair a final swipe, then tucked her brush into a small blue shoulder bag, along with a lipstick and coin purse.

Jack watched her golden hair cascade over her shoulders, stared at the glossy, parted fullness of her lips. He ached to touch her. "Let's go," he said gruffly. "It's about a half-hour drive, and we're already running late."

He strode several feet ahead of her down the two flights of stairs to the main entrance of the building, letting the heavy door in the vestibule slam shut before she reached it. Grimacing, Colleen pushed it open and followed him to the adjacent parking lot. He climbed into a sporty black Pontiac Firebird, slid behind the wheel, and gave the horn an impudent honk as Colleen wobbled across the gravel in her high, narrow heels.

The wind was blowing and the temperature seemed to have dropped at least twenty degrees since the afternoon. Colleen shivered. She definitely should have worn a coat, but *he* had advised against it. Invigorating, he'd said. Maybe to a polar bear!

He didn't even bother to reach across the seat to open the door for her. Colleen's brown eyes were blazing as she flung open the door and climbed inside. She was fumbling for the clasp of her seat belt when Jack gunned the engine and the car lurched forward. Colleen lurched forward, too, bracing her hands on the dashboard. She glowered over at him. The man had the manners of a Neanderthal!

"It's a good thing this is a faux date," she said. "Otherwise, it would be over right now."

"The charade doesn't begin until we're in the presence of my mother and my aunts." Jack knew he was behaving abominably. For reasons he didn't care to examine further, he didn't dare act any other way.

"Nicola thinks this whole idea is dumb," Colleen said tightly. "She says we won't fool anybody, that you can't act what you don't feel."

"I disagree. Did you ever read William James's theory in Psych 101? He believed that actions govern feelings rather than the reverse."

Colleen's eyes widened. "So if we *act* as if we're in love, we'll end up feeling that we're in love?" She frowned. "Maybe we'd better rethink this whole plan. I don't want to fall in love with a cold-blooded fortune hunter."

"And I have no intention of falling in love with an idealistic little virgin without a fortune. William James to the contrary, we're both quite safe from each other's charms, Colleen."

Colleen had never heard anyone sound so adamant about anything.

Jack slowed the car to a stop at a red light and shot her a coolly appraising glance. "Don't even think about trying to back out now, Colleen. You agreed to play the part of my sweet little lady love and you're going to do it—and convincingly, too."

"This is sounding less like a favor and more like a command. I don't *have* to do it, you know, Jack. You're my boss during working hours only, and even then, only when I'm working on a column—which I have yet to do, because you won't give me a chance to write one."

"I already have ten columns written and ready to use, so I don't need anything written by an assistant."

"I bet you never will, either. You have no intention of ever letting me write a column for you, so you'll always keep at least ten columns on hand."

"You may be right. If you don't like it, ask Kazorowski to assign you permanently to the women's pages."

"They aren't called women's pages anymore. They haven't been since the late sixties," Colleen retorted.

"Oh yeah, they renamed that section 'Lifestyle' or 'Living,' and it's supposed to appeal to everybody. Except it doesn't. It's still of interest strictly to women."

"You're wrong, but I'm not going to waste my

energy arguing with you." He excelled at riling her, Colleen silently admitted. Her best bet would be to ignore him. She stared purposefully out the window.

And then she crossed her legs. Jack caught a fleeting glimpse of a lacy white slip and heard the soft rustling of one nylon-clad thigh moving against the other. His heartbeat accelerated and a rush of sexual heat suffused him. Once again he was catapulted back into the realm of erotic fantasy with Colleen Brady as his leading lady.

He wanted her; there was no use trying to deny it. But he couldn't have her, because she was definitely not the type to enjoy great sex without any strings attached. Only a good-time action-girl accepted an affair on those terms; sweet young virgins spun a tighter web than a spider. Their demands for love, commitment, marriage, and family bound a man like steel threads.

Jack reminded himself how much he cherished his freedom and independence; he remembered his ambition to marry rich. An affair with Colleen Brady clashed with both his goals. Yet knowing all that, here he sat, hard and hungry for her. Tonight was a big mistake, he could see that now.

"You know, maybe your friend Nicola has a point after all. How can I—" He broke off abruptly. *How can I act like a chaste gentleman all evening when what I really feel like doing is tearing off that silky little dress and—*

He didn't dare let himself finish that potent thought. Fortunately, the light turned green and he had to turn his full attention to the road.

"You were about to say how can you act like you're in love with me when you don't even like me?" surmised Colleen. "I think we're about to shoot William James's as-if theory down in flames."

Jack was not about to confess that he was caught in the powerful throes of lust for her. One did not supply the enemy with weapons! "It's such a ridicu-

lous situation," he growled, "having to pretend to be
involved with you when you're not my type and
never will be, never could be, never would be . . ."

He recognized that he was protesting too much
and immediately lapsed into silence. What a relief
that Colleen hadn't picked up on it! He realized,
with a flash of insight, that she hadn't because she
didn't recognize her own feminine power. Colleen
Brady looked in the mirror every day and had to
know that she was attractive, but she had no idea
of how sexually appealing she was. She was innocent and unawakened and completely unaware that
a man could want her as badly as he did at this
moment.

Which was certainly lucky for him! Jack breathed
a sigh of relief.

Colleen heard his sigh and assumed it was one
of impatience, of disgust at finding himself in this
"ridiculous situation."

"Well, this stupid charade of a date wasn't my
idea, it was yours, remember?" she said defensively.
"And if you don't want to go through with it, it's
fine with me. You can take me home. It turns out
that I have something to do tonight after all."

"And what's that? A blind date with another guy
who doesn't speak English and spends the evening
asleep in his plate?"

Colleen scowled. She was sorry she'd ever mentioned her ill-fated date to him. "You don't think it's
possible for me to have a date with someone who
knows and likes me?"

Oh, it was possible, all right. Quite possible. And
the prospect sent a hot surge of anger coursing
through him. Which he chose to take out on her.
"Correct me if I'm wrong, but the two dates you've
had since moving to Buffalo have been a blind date
with that guy from Afghanistan and this contrived
one with me. Repressed little virgins are not hot
commodities in the dating market, Colleen."

Colleen lifted her chin to a regal tilt. His remark

stung, but she would not let him know. "My date the other night was from Pakistan," she said haughtily.

"Pakistan. I stand corrected."

They drove in silence for what seemed an eternity, though the clock on the dashboard showed that less than ten minutes had elapsed. "So what else could you be doing tonight?" Jack asked at last. His voice seemed to echo in the stillness.

"Working," Colleen replied at once. The silence had been getting to her; she'd wanted to end it herself, but wasn't sure how. "I saw *Meatgrinder Massacre* this afternoon, and I have to finish up my review for tomorrow's edition."

"*Meatgrinder Massacre?*" Jack grinned despite himself. "You're joking, right?"

"I wish I were. It's one hundred and eleven minutes of blood, gore, and violence. No plot, no characterization, just scene after scene of a maniacal meatgrinder and its luckless victims. I'm not a very knowledgeable film critic, but you don't have to be one to know when a movie is completely atrocious."

"A maniacal meatgrinder on the loose, hm? It'll undoubtedly be a smash hit with the movie-going teen set. I hope you're prepared to review *Meatgrinder Massacre* parts two, three, and four. Hey, there could be *Meatgrinder Massacre*s to infinity."

Colleen groaned. Jack laughed.

"Here's the Rainbow Bridge," he announced, slowing to a stop. "The U.S.–Canadian border."

Colleen looked around, her brown eyes glowing with interest. "I've never been out of the United States before, not even to Mexico when I was living in Texas. And I can't wait to see Niagara Falls."

Having grown up in Buffalo, Jack took the Falls for granted, but he had a certain native's pride in showing them off to a wide-eyed tourist. "It's quite a sight, seeing them for the first time. You'll be able to see both the American and Canadian falls from the restaurant."

The border guard waved them through, and they drove across the high-level bridge from Niagara Falls, New York, to Niagara Falls, Canada. The horseshoe-shaped Canadian falls were visible as Jack steered the car into a wide parking lot, adjacent to the hotel housing the restaurant.

"They're incredible!" Colleen exclaimed. "I wish we could go closer."

Jack grabbed her wrist and propelled her into the self-service elevator. "You'll have a better view from the top."

They were the only two people in the elevator. Colleen's eyes darted to her wrist, manacled by Jack's long fingers. A man of his size and strength and power could make her do anything he wanted her to do. For one unguarded moment, she found such feminine helplessness intriguing.

Colleen instantly rebuked herself. She was a woman of the nineties, not a nitwit who found romance in a caveman mentality. And this particular caveman had a self-admitted penchant for gold digging.

So why did she find him so fascinating? Colleen wondered a little wildly. He had more faults than any man she'd ever dated; he was arrogant and insulting . . . yet whenever he threw a crumb to her, she forgot the animosity smoldering between them and inexplicably responded to him.

Jack was still holding on to her when the elevator doors snapped shut and the car began its rapid ascent. "You're hurting my wrist," Colleen said coolly. He wasn't. But this peculiar tension strumming through her was unnerving enough to make her lie.

"Am I?" His voice was deep and low. He loosened his grip a little and began to move his thumb slowly and lightly across her palm.

Colleen felt a quiver deep in her belly. "Don't," she said breathlessly.

"Your hand is trembling, Colleen." Jack entwined his fingers with hers. "Why, I wonder?"

She snatched her hand away. "Maybe it's because I'm claustrophobic and riding in an elevator."

"Excellent, Colleen." Jack laughed appreciatively. "You can think fast on your feet. I admire verbal acuity."

He gazed down at her. A flush tinged her delicate skin; he'd felt the racing pulse beat as he'd held her wrist. He was too experienced not to recognize the subtle signs and read them for what they were—sexual awareness and the beginnings of arousal. His loins throbbed in response and a reckless elation coursed through him.

"Shall we get in character right now?" His dark eyes glittered. "What would a madly-in-love couple do if they found themselves alone in an elevator?"

"They'd make small talk," Colleen said quickly. "Because she would be nervous about meeting his family for the first time, so he would try to reassure her."

"Wrong answer, Colleen." How could he be irritated and aroused at the same time? he wondered. And each condition seemed to heighten the other. "No wonder you're still a virgin. A woman with a modicum of passion would instinctively know when to stop talking and when to start—"

"Groping and pawing?" She wrenched her hand from his. "Maybe I don't have a modicum of passion, but I have lots of common sense. And I'm not about to start necking with you in elevators, knowing what I do about you."

"And what do you know about me?"

"I know that you're a user, with the depth and sensitivity of—of a *Meatgrinder Massacre* script."

Jack laughed. "The little duckling strikes back. I know I'm supposed to take offense, but I commend your originality. I've been compared to a rat and a snake, but this is the first time I've been—"

"I meant to lance that oversize ego of yours, not make you laugh," Colleen interrupted, frowning.

"And I was entertained instead of insulted. Poor Colleen."

The elevator doors opened to a brightly lit corridor. "This is it." Jack cupped her elbow in his hand and guided her toward a set of double glass doors. He opened the door for her and held it open until she passed, then followed her through it.

"Your mother must be watching," Colleen remarked dryly. "Otherwise, you'd've rushed ahead of me and let the door slam in my face."

"She's at the table on the left, by the window, watching every move we make," Jack said, smiling through gritted teeth. "Mom's in red, Aunt Judy is in blue, and Aunt Dorothy is in yellow."

"How convenient. They came color-coded."

Jack's fixed smile turned into a real one. "Behave, Colleen. You're supposed to be adoring, not clever."

"You want me to simper and sigh and hang on your every word?"

"Yeah, that would do nicely."

"Then this is going to be a very long evening."

"Oh, and Colleen, we're supposed to be seriously involved, remember? That means we've known each other longer than a few days. If anybody asks, you'll have to say you've been living in Buffalo for a while."

"How long?" They were nearing the table. Jack's mother and aunts stood up and hurried to meet them.

"I don't know. Six months? A year?" Jack hissed just before Aunt Judy, the one all in blue, grabbed them both for a double bear hug.

He made the introductions, and the group stood and talked for a while in the middle of the restaurant. Nobody seemed to mind; the clientele was largely tourists who were roaming around, snapping pictures of the Falls from every angle. A large group of children seated at a long table at one end of the room were noisily entertaining each other.

Just as he'd predicted, his relatives fell in love with Colleen on sight. And Colleen was charming to them, smiling, sweet and spontaneous, saying exactly the right things.

"She's darling, Jack!" Aunt Dorothy exclaimed effusively. "Just adorable!"

His mother was positively beaming. "So different from Don—"

"Now, Helen, let the past be," Judy admonished her sister. Her voice lowered to a whisper, which everyone heard anyway. "We don't know what Colleen knows about you-know-who."

"Oh, I know all about Donna, that baseball-happy little hustler," Colleen said with an ingenuous smile. She heard Jack draw a sharp breath, and her smile widened. "Jack told me about her and their marriage and divorce."

Helen Blackledge leaned closer, her tone becoming conspiratorial. "We were all so worried about him after—"

"Mom!" Jack interjected sharply. He sent Colleen a look of mute desperation. Her eyes were sparkling, as if she were holding back laughter. He clenched his jaw. "Why don't we sit down now?" It was more an order than a suggestion.

Helen took Colleen's hand. "Sit here, dear, between Jack and me." They all took their seats at the table by the window. "Are you a native of Buffalo? How did you meet Jack?" Jack's mother fired the questions without pausing to breathe.

Before Colleen could answer, Aunt Dorothy chimed in with, "How long have you two been dating?"

"Six months," said Colleen at the same time that Jack said, "About a year."

They looked at each other and exchanged pained glances.

"Six months? A year? Which is it?" demanded Aunt Judy.

Jack's talent for romantic fiction—limited to begin

with—failed him completely. He grabbed his water glass and began to gulp down the contents.

Colleen squared her shoulders and plunged ahead. "Well, it sort of depends. Jack told me he fell in love with me at first sight when we met at the paper a year ago just after I came to Buffalo, so he says we've been together for a year." Her velvety brown eyes gleamed. "But since he pined away for me in silence for six whole months because he didn't have the courage to ask me out, I start counting from our first date, which was six months ago."

Jack nearly choked on his water. "Colleen," his voice held a warning note.

"He gets embarrassed when I tell that story, because I was the first woman he's ever been shy with," Colleen continued blithely.

"I could have predicted it," Aunt Dorothy cried triumphantly. "I always knew that when our Jack really fell in love, he would be totally different from that cocky, young smart aleck he pretends to be."

"No, he's certainly not a cocky, young smart aleck around me," said Colleen. "He's sensitive and sweet and gentle." She searched for additional adjectives to describe this feminist dream-man who would be, of course, a nightmare to macho Jack.

"Sensitive, sweet, and gentle?" Jack echoed. He sounded appalled. Colleen grinned. He frowned.

"He's thoughtful, and he never forgets a birthday or anniversary," Colleen continued grandly. "He's always giving me candy and flowers and special little presents and—he cries during sad movies," she finished with a flourish.

"*Cries?*" Jack interrupted, completely horrified. "*Me?*" His mother and aunts were staring at him, and he managed a killing smile. "That's my little Colleen—such a kidder. As you three well know, I haven't cried since my nursery-school days."

"He's so sensitive he gets embarrassed about it," Colleen confided.

"I'm so glad he's been able to express his feelings

with you, Colleen," his mother said earnestly. "Jack's father was a wonderful man, but he was a firm believer in the men-shouldn't-cry school of thought and he had Jack believing it from the age of four. Why, Jack wouldn't even cry at his father's funeral thirteen years ago—'Dad wouldn't want me to,' he said."

"We definitely express our feelings," Colleen assured her. "All the time." She ignored Jack's kick under the table.

His mother and the aunts were enraptured. They took turns telling Colleen how they'd always known that the right woman would be able to penetrate their dear Jack's facade of indifference. Since Colleen had done so, she was clearly, obviously the ideal mate for their boy.

There was a piano and small dance-band combo in the corner of the room, and the musicians began to play during the lull between the Blackledge party's appetizers and main course.

"That's one of my favorite songs," Helen Blackledge said, reminiscing. " 'Lady in Red.' So romantic, so moving."

"It's sentimental, banal, and absurd," Jack muttered under his breath.

Colleen chuckled. "There's definitely a musical generation gap here."

"Colleen, Jack, you two should dance," proclaimed Aunt Dorothy. "The candlelight, the music, the Falls in the background . . . the atmosphere is just perfect."

"Too bad Colleen's trick knee has been acting up," Jack said smoothly. "No dancing for us."

"Oh, what a shame." Aunt Judy's face fell. "We just love to see young people dancing."

Colleen stood up. "Remember those warm compresses and the aspirin the doctor recommended, Jack? Well, they worked. My knee is as good as new. We can dance after all."

"Forget it," growled Jack.

"But you're such a good dancer, Jack!" his mother protested. "Remember those ballroom dancing lessons you took at Miss Wilcroft's Academy of Dance? I don't think we've seen you dance since the sixth grade," she added wistfully.

"Come on, Jack, just one dance," said Colleen, tugging on the sleeve of his jacket. There was an unholy gleam in her eyes. "Surely you can dredge up a memory of the old box step."

"Oh, for goodness' sake!" Jack tossed his napkin onto the table and rose from his chair. "One dance, and then I don't want to hear the word mentioned again."

They walked to the small dance floor as the three sisters beamed their approval.

Five

"You're having a terrific time portraying me as a wimpy sap, aren't you, Colleen?" Jack practically growled as he took her in his arms. "You're so very pleased with yourself."

"I like making people happy. And look how happy they are, Jack." Colleen smiled and waved at the enthusiastic trio at the table. All three women waved back. "So you took ballroom dancing lessons?" She tilted her head and laughed up at him. "You dance quite well. Miss Wilcroft would be proud of you."

They were dancing very properly, her right hand in his, her left resting on his shoulder. His big hand was splayed lightly across her back. Their bodies weren't close enough to touch; in fact, there was room for a third party in the space between them.

"Miss Wilcroft was a two hundred-eighty-pound gargoyle, and those stupid lessons were pure hell for a kid who lived and breathed baseball. I refused to dance at all for years afterward. I took it up again when I realized the advantages of slow dancing as a prelude to getting a woman in bed."

Jack felt her tense and smiled wolfishly. She'd been teasing him unmercifully in front of his relatives, and it was time for a bit of good old-fashioned revenge. "Of course, what we're doing now doesn't come close to some of the X-rated scenes I've played on the dance floor. Shall I demonstrate the difference?"

X-rated dancing? Colleen's heart jumped. "No! We have a G-rated audience, remember?"

"You wanted to make them happy," Jack reminded her mockingly. "Well, those three starry-eyed romantics are about to be transported to the realms of ecstasy."

With one easy movement, he pulled her against him. He wanted to hold her, and one dance under the watchful eyes of his mother and aunts hardly constituted any danger, Jack assured himself. "Put your arms around my neck," he ordered as he linked his arms tightly around her waist.

There was really nowhere else for her arms to go, Colleen realized dizzily, because their bodies were molded together so tightly that she couldn't possibly have wedged her arms between them. And she could hardly let them dangle loose and straight at her sides, not unless she cared to give explanations to the threesome ogling them from the table. Hesitantly, feeling utterly trapped, she laid her hands on his shoulders, not daring to curve her arms around him.

They were so close that there wasn't an inch of her not touching him, yet somehow he pressed even closer. Colleen drew in a sharp gulp of air. She could feel the solid, muscular heat of him imprinted against the length of her whole body; she could feel his breath in her hair.

"Relax," Jack breathed against her ear. "You're too stiff. I feel as if I'm dancing with a broomstick. Well, not exactly," he amended with a deep chuckle. "You're too soft and rounded in certain places to qualify as a bona fide broomstick. But you definitely need to loosen up."

"I—I'm always stiff when I dance," Colleen mumbled. He was so big and warm and strong. She felt a disconcerting urge to close her eyes and melt into his hard male frame. She stumbled slightly. He tightened his hold protectively, and she felt her head begin to spin.

"I'm not a very good dancer. I keep worrying I'll end up crippling my partner by tramping all over his feet." She'd never been clumsy, nor had she ever had difficulty slow dancing until now. Maybe her words were prophetic, for the sharp high heel of her shoe nearly punctured his foot. Jack deftly stepped out of range. "See what I mean?" Colleen asked with a nervous little laugh.

She waited for him to razz her about having two left feet. The last thing she expected was for him to cup the nape of her neck with his big hand and begin a slow massage with his fingers.

"You're doing fine," he murmured softly. With his other hand, which was resting on the small of her back, he began to knead the sensitive hollow of her spine. It was an area of her body Colleen had been totally unaware of until this moment, but it was proving to be a powerfully erogenous one. Her body felt as if it had just burst into flames.

In fact, every nerve in her body was responding to his sensuous caresses. Her skin felt feverish, and ribbons of heat rippled through her. Her breasts, crushed against the muscular wall of Jack's chest, felt heavy and full, her nipples tingled and grew taut. A powerful, instinctive urge to rub against him sent her reeling. There was a pounding in her ears that pulsed in harmony with the shameful, forbidden, exciting throbbing between her thighs.

Her tension and inhibitions melted like hot honey, and she relaxed, her curvy softness flowing against the hard masculine planes of his body. There were no more stumbles, no more near misses with her stilettolike heels. She was moving in perfect time to the slow, dreamy music, her body swaying against his in their own mutual rhythm. Colleen's eyelids drooped and then closed as she drew a deep, shuddering breath.

Jack was hard and heavy and stirring against her. But instead of shrinking from his blatant masculinity, Colleen wriggled closer. She'd never felt so vibrantly sexual, had never been so vitally aware of her own femininity. When she felt his lips on the curve of her neck, a breathless sigh escaped from her throat.

"Jack." She whispered his name, lost in a sensual dream world. He was nibbling on her neck and caressing her, and the desire surging through her was a raging tide. She tilted her head to one side to give him better access to her throat, and sighed again.

Jack's senses rioted. He drew a steadying breath, but when he inhaled, the sexy, elusive scent of her perfume went straight to his head like a shot of hundred-proof whiskey, clouding his mind. She felt so small and soft and warm in his arms. And though their bodies were as close as they could possibly be, he wanted to be even closer, without the restrictions of clothing, feeling her sleek, silken skin bare against him. He picture himself removing that proper little dress of hers and feeling her naked and responsive as he moved against her . . .

The slow song ended and the band struck up a raucous version of the decidedly unromantic theme from *Ghostbusters*. The children at the long table provided the vocals at top volume. Stunned and dazed, Colleen and Jack drew apart and stared at each other. Neither spoke. Both were flushed and breathing heavily.

"Jack! Hey, Jack!" The jovial male voice seemed to come from another dimension.

Jack and Colleen simultaneously turned toward the sound. A tall, strapping man with a shock of blond hair was loping toward them.

"Oh no!" Jack groaned.

"Wh—who is it?" Colleen stammered. It was surprisingly difficult to talk. Her mind was so fogged that it was an effort to find the right words, and her mouth was trembling. The loud music and the children's boisterous yells lent a surreal element to the scene.

"Hey, Blackie, it *is* you." The blond giant gave Jack a hearty slap on the back. "I thought so, but I could hardly believe my own eyes. What are you doing *here*? This place sure as hell isn't your usual scene." He gave a ribald laugh, then his eyes roamed speculatively over Colleen. His wide grin faded to an expression of puzzled disbelief. "She sure as hell isn't your usual choice of babe—uh, lady, either. Hey pal, what gives?"

Colleen stared from Jack's appalled countenance to the blond man's incredulous one. The passion she'd felt while in Jack's arms drained from her as abruptly as water from a sink whose stopper had been removed. *Usual choice of babe*. The phrase rang in her ears. It reminded her that she was back in the real world, the world where Jack Blackledge's female companions were unfit to be presented to his mother and aunts. The world in which he considered money to be the first and foremost reason for marriage.

A horrifyingly vivid memory of how she'd been dancing with him flashed before her mind's eye. The way she'd been plastered up against him, the way she'd been moving and feeling . . . all those things *he'd* made her feel! Colleen flushed scarlet from her cheeks to the tips of her toes.

"Hey, what's with you two? You been struck dumb or something?" the big muscle-bound blond demanded.

"Or something, I guess," Colleen replied. She was back in full command of her wits now. The temporary insanity that had possessed her during that wanton, intimate dance had mercifully passed. "I'm Colleen Brady," she said to the man, offering her hand to shake. "I work with Jack at the *Times-Gazette*, and you happened to catch us during our act. We were trying to pretend that we're in love for the benefit of Jack's mother and aunts. Were we convincing?"

"Rodd Garrett." The blond man lifted Colleen's hand to his lips and kissed her fingertips, continental style. The gesture seemed ludicrously at odds with his hulking physique. "Yeah, you were convincing. It was a scary sight. I figured when a guy like Black Jack cuddles up with a nice girl in a family-type place, it can only mean one thing—that marriage is looming."

Jack watched the interaction through cloudy eyes. Garrett had yet to release Colleen's hand, he noted sourly. And she was animated as always; her expressive brown eyes were gleaming with humor as she joked with Rodd Garrett about the absurd notion that she could be involved with Jack Blackledge.

It annoyed him that Colleen had recovered so quickly, so completely, while he was still rigid with sexual tension. His mind was taking a singularly long time to clear. He found it galling that she was smiling and laughing and flirting—yes, she was definitely flirting!—while he stood mute, trying to gather his wits.

"This isn't exactly your scene either, Garrett," Jack interjected with a bit of a snarl. "Who are you here with?"

Rodd Garrett grinned. "Hear that mob of kiddies screaming the *Ghostbusters* song at the top of their little lungs?"

"We'd be stone-deaf if we didn't," Jack growled.

"Well, I'm with them. It's my nephew's birthday party—y'know, he's my sister Rita's kid. The boy idolizes me. He's always bragging about his uncle Rodd, who plays with the Buffalo Bills." Rodd Garrett shrugged. "You know how kids are. I couldn't disappoint the little guy."

"That's very kind of you," Colleen said warmly. "What position do you play with the Bills?"

"Offensive lineman," Rodd told her. He went on to

talk about the team and his role in it. Colleen listened attentively.

Garrett hadn't bothered to mention that he was not a starter or that he'd nearly been cut by the team this season, Jack noted darkly. But that probably wouldn't have made a difference to Colleen anyway. After all, Rodd Garrett was a professional athlete, albeit a fading one, and Jack knew all about the fascination professional athletes held for women. He'd once traded on it as unabashedly as Rodd Garrett still did. For a few moments Jack stood and listened to them, feeling ignored and, in turn, outraged by the exclusion.

"You're a genuine smooth operator, Garrett." Jack finally injected himself in the conversation. "First you drop the doting uncle bit to soften her up, then you casually throw in that you're a pro football player to impress the hell out of her."

Colleen and Rodd turned to stare at him, and Jack felt a dark flush stain his neck. The bitterness in his tone had surprised him too. He forced a smile, determined to cover his telltale lapse. "Come on over and say hello to my mother and aunts, Rodd. They'll be thrilled to see you."

He placed a fraternal hand on Rodd's shoulder and steered him over to the table, where the sisters were indeed delighted to see Jack's old friend once again.

"We went to the same high school, though ol' Black Jack was a couple years ahead of me," Rodd told Colleen while the others reminisced about the good old days. "For a few years we were both riding high, the heroes of the old neighborhood, with pro-ball contracts and—" he broke off.

Colleen glanced quickly from one man to the other as the awkward pause lengthened. Jack Blackledge's pro career had been cut short by injury, while Rodd Garrett's was still going strong. She considered the full impact that the long-ago car accident had had on Jack's life. The changes it had brought were as profound as those in her own life after the Bradys' fateful meeting with the overwhelming Ramsey clan. But both she and Jack had successfully met the challenge of building an entirely new life. They had more in common than it might appear, she concluded thoughtfully.

She stole another peek at Jack and found his eyes resting on her. A frisson of heat quivered through her as she remembered the feel of his body against hers, his big caressing hands, his mouth hot against her neck . . .

Jack looked away first, breaking the invisible chain that locked their gazes together. Colleen felt an odd sense of regret as she turned her attention back to Rodd and the ladies.

"But hey, Jack is the smart one," Rodd was saying expansively, his voice perhaps a bit too hearty. "He got himself a great career with the newspaper while I'm still getting pounded on the ball field. Which brings me to that column you wrote the other day, Blackie, the one where you accused the NFL players' union of being as greedy as the owners. . . . What kind of slanderous, traitorous bull is that, buddy?"

The two men argued good-naturedly about the wisdom of a football strike as the main course was served. Rodd Garrett remained at their table for the rest of the evening, with occasional time-outs for visits to his nephew's birthday party.

"Isn't it nice that Colleen and Rodd get along so well?" Helen Blackledge remarked as she, her sisters, and Jack watched Rodd pull a protesting, laughing Colleen onto the dance floor for the third time. "I imagine the two of you see a lot of him. Any chance of Rodd settling down with a nice girl like Colleen? It would make his mother so happy, I know."

Jack made no reply, but he was frowning. From Rodd's behavior, it seemed as if he wouldn't mind settling down with Colleen herself. He'd been practically drooling over her since they'd met. Nor was Jack fooled by his pal's presence at their table. Rodd

Garrett hadn't joined them to indulge in a nostalgic evening with his former neighbors; he wasn't there to banter with his good buddy Jack, or even to escape from his nephew's tiresome birthday festivities. Rodd Garrett had joined the Blackledge party for one reason only—to come on to Colleen.

Jack's mood grew darker as the evening progressed. Every time he looked at Colleen and Rodd together an unexpected feeling of betrayal coursed through him. And it was appalling to him. Yet telling himself that he had no right or reason to feel that way didn't erase the feelings.

Rodd stayed after his nephew's birthday party was over. He danced with each of the widows, and he danced several more times with Colleen. Jack didn't. He remained in his seat, talking to his mother and aunts about the shop in Orlando, about his four married cousins, Judy's and Dorothy's daughters, who lived in Florida with their families, about Buffalo's position as the country's flour-milling capital, and the National Park service's plan to preserve the city's oldest grain elevators as historic national parks.

Never had he played the part of dutiful son and nephew so zealously. Any topic was a welcome distraction from watching Rodd and Colleen laugh and dance and carry on like a couple of giddy teenagers.

It was past eleven when Jack, Colleen, and Rodd walked the three sisters to their rented car and waved them off.

"Hey, Jack, show's over. No need to carry on with your charade now. Why don't I drive Colleen home?" Rodd suggested with a brashness that made Jack want to clobber him.

"I brought her here, I'll take her home," Jack said. He snatched Colleen's hand in what he knew was an entirely inappropriate proprietary gesture. And he didn't release her.

"I've got my Ferrari," Rodd said, his eyes bright with triumph. He was clearly playing what he con-

considered his trump card and waited expectantly for Colleen's excited acquiescence to his offer.

Colleen didn't react at all. The Ramseys were sports car aficionados, and she'd spent the past seven years among the most exotic, expensive sports cars in the world. She wasn't bowled over by a chance to ride in a Ferrari. She was far more intrigued by Jack's determination to keep her from riding in it. She opted to go home with him instead.

"Why didn't you want me to ride home with Rodd?" she asked Jack as they drove back across the bridge. Rodd Garrett had left alone in his red Ferrari.

"Call it a quixotic whim," replied Jack. Triumph vibrated through him. He felt exhilarated every time he thought of Colleen choosing him and his Firebird over Rodd and his Ferrari, but he didn't bother to analyze why. "A guy like Rodd Garrett is no match for a wide-eyed innocent like you."

"It seems to me that I'm in a lot more danger around you," Colleen retorted. "Rodd wasn't the one who made a heavy pass at me on the dance floor." She was a little astonished at her own bluntness, but she found she needed to discuss what had happened between them that evening. Had it meant anything at all to him?

"You were with me all the way, baby," Jack shot back.

Colleen blushed. On second thought, maybe she didn't want to talk about it after all. "I like your mother and aunts," she said quickly, striving for safe ground. "They're very nice ladies."

"Yeah, they are."

"And they adore you."

He smiled. "They're pretty crazy about you too. Colleen, I, uh, want to thank you for tonight. You did make them happy, and I appreciate it."

Colleen merely nodded. *If only it were true.* The unbidden wistful thought flashed through her mind.

But it wasn't, the realist inside her reminded her frankly. They'd been role-playing tonight, and she didn't dare ignore fact and slip into fantasy. That was a guaranteed prescription for disaster.

"Did Rodd ask you out?"

Jack's voice filtered through her thoughts. His voice was so matter-of-fact, his question so casual that she replied in kind. "Yes, to a party a week from this Friday."

"Did you tell him you'd go?"

"I told him to call me, and I'd let him know."

"Clever, Colleen. You know just how to bait the hook, hm? You're fully aware that a guy like Rodd has his pick of women, so making yourself a challenge is a surefire way to—"

"I wasn't plotting out any grand strategy!" Colleen interrupted hotly. "I don't play those games. I said I'd let him know because I'm not sure I want to go to the party with him."

"Why not? You obviously like the guy. I spent most of the evening watching you bat your eyes at him and listening to you charm him with your girlish giggles. I'll bet you can't wait to tell your roommate that you've landed a date with Rodd Garrett. He's one of the most eligible bachelors in Buffalo, you know."

"No, I didn't know, nor do I care. And I was *not* batting my eyes at him or . . . giggling girlishly!"

"I've watched women make fools of themselves over pro athletes for years. It's a common syndrome—women throwing themselves at celebrities. There are rock groupies and baseball Annies and—"

"I did not throw myself at Rodd Garrett!" Colleen cut in sharply. She was seething, yet there was an uneasy streak of anxiety mingled with her anger. Had Rodd Garrett misinterpreted her behavior as Jack had? She found it ironic that Jack had mistaken her friendliness toward Rodd for attraction. The truth was she'd been so attuned to Jack all evening that she'd been operating on automatic pilot with everyone else.

"I'm not a sports fan and I'm not overly impressed with football players—or with former baseball players," she added crossly.

"But, of course, you'll go to the party with Rodd. The woman who turns down a date with an eligible pro football player who owns a Ferrari has yet to be born."

"Not true! You're looking at her!"

"I'll believe it when you actually say no to the guy," Jack drawled sardonically.

"Which I will do as soon as he calls," Colleen snapped. "You're the gold digger, not me."

Feeling extraordinarily pleased with himself, Jack flashed her a smile. He made a few desultory attempts at conversation during the rest of the drive but gave up when she answered him only in monosyllables.

Remembering their every-man-for-himself departure from the apartment earlier, Colleen fully expected Jack to pull up in front of the building, impatiently idle the engine while she climbed out of the car, and then peel off into the night. She was astonished when he escorted her to her door and unlocked it for her.

"Well." Colleen stood on the threshold and stared down at the rubber mat. A sudden tension gripped her. All her senses seemed to go on alert, and she was acutely aware of Jack standing close at her side. "It was certainly an . . . interesting evening."

"Yes, wasn't it?"

She stepped backward into the apartment, which was completely dark. Her heart began to pound wildly when he followed her in and pulled the door closed behind him. "I—I guess Nic and I both forgot to leave a light on," she stammered, and her voice was thin from nerves. "Or maybe she's back and has gone to bed. There—there is a switch on that wall— oh!"

She didn't see him reach for her, but she felt the controlled strength of his arms pulling her to him, felt the solid heat of his body impact against her. And then his mouth was on hers.

If any other man had grabbed her in the dark, she would have panicked and fought off his advances. But when Jack's lips met hers, she welcomed him. Her senses spun wildly. It was as if the hours between this moment and the burgeoning arousal she'd experienced in his arms on the dance floor hadn't occurred. She was primed for him. Hungry for him.

She moaned when his tongue touched hers and tilted her head back to fully accept the power of his scorching kiss. Her arms crept around his neck and she clung to him, her anchor in the dark, swirling sea of sensuality.

Jack held her closer, arching her to him as his tongue probed her mouth, and she quivered with a sweet heated pleasure at the deepening intimacy of the kiss. With a deft, experienced move, he covered her breast with his hand.

The sensation was electrifying. Colleen gasped a shuddering breath as she felt the heat of his big hand cupping her, his long fingers beginning a slow, sensuous massage. He rubbed her nipple, which had already peaked and was achingly sensitive, sending hot little sparks to the most secret, feminine part of her.

He was boldly, fully aroused, his hard flesh pressing insistently against her. A syrupy warmth flowed through her, leaving her weak and soft and pliant. When he slid his hands down to knead and cup her buttocks before lifting her high and hard against him, an uncontrollably erotic spasm convulsed her. She felt him between her legs where her womanhood was swollen and hot and throbbing. She'd never experienced such a burning, writhing need and the intensity of it both shocked and excited her.

He was kissing her as she'd never been kissed

before, hard and deep and intimate, his tongue moving in and out of her mouth in excruciating sexual simulation, demanding and receiving her body's most primitive, passionate responses . . .

Later, alone in her room that night, Colleen would toss and turn and wonder just how far their passion would have carried them if there hadn't been a sudden, shocking blaze of light accompanied by a startled gasp.

"Oops!" The exclamation was followed by an embarrassed giggle.

It took Jack and Colleen several disoriented seconds before they comprehended that they were no longer alone, that someone had switched on the overhead light, had gasped and giggled nervously. Nicola.

Jack dropped his arms and moved speedily away from Colleen, as if distancing himself from something radioactive. Colleen placed a bracing hand against the wall; her limbs were so weak and shaky she was afraid she might fall.

"I'm so sorry!" Nicola exclaimed. "I had no idea . . ." Her voice trailed off, then she cleared her throat and ventured in a comically polite tone, "Kamal, you already know Colleen. I'd like you to meet Jack Blackledge, her, er, boss?"

Jack swore soundlessly. His body was shaking from the intensity of their passion and from its abrupt cessation; his breathing was heavy and thick. His gaze swept reflexively over Colleen, who was standing against the wall, her face flushed and downcast, her big brown eyes glistening.

"Very pleased to meet you, Mr. Blackledge." A wry young man with a shock of dark, thick hair and a black mustache extended his hand for Jack to shake. "Kamal Veli," he gave his name. "We apologize for the untimely interruption. Nicola invited me up for coffee. Perhaps you will join us?"

Jack admired the younger man's aplomb. Did medical training prepare one to handle all sorts of scenes? He shook Kamal Veli's hand and managed a wan smile. "Maybe it wasn't so untimely," he murmured.

Maybe Nicola and Kamal's appearance had been downright providential, he thought. The way he'd been feeling, that incredible intensity of passion, almost painful in its pleasure . . . the raging demands of his body . . . Colleen's impassioned responses and implicit surrender . . .

He couldn't remember the last time he'd been turned on so fast and so hard—and they'd only been kissing! Uninterrupted, they would've ended up in bed, he was certain of it. And taking the virginal, bewitching, and captivating Colleen to bed could never be an end in itself, it would be a beginning. *The beginning of the real-life version of the scene they'd played tonight for his family.* Serious involvement, marriage, children who had noisy birthday parties . . .

He began to perspire. He felt as if he were free-falling into a black hole. A relationship with Colleen would mean intimacy and emotional engagement, the type of bonding that he had no intention of ever risking. But Colleen would need that sort of commitment; she would demand it. And that was her right. But he was a guy who lived on the surface, coasting along, indifferent and detached. *Give him superficial or give him death*—or words to that effect. That was *his* right.

Jack stared at Colleen, who hadn't looked up once since Nicola and Kamal's unexpected arrival. He was unnerved by how much he wanted to put his arms around her and soothe her distress. If he did, the evening would end with the two of them sharing coffee and conversation with Nicola and Kamal, the awkward moment smoothed over and put behind them, their relationship moving ahead into the uncharted waters of depth and promises and vows. . .

"Hey, it's late. Gotta be up by six." Jack went to

the door like someone fleeing an apparition. "Can't stay for coffee, but it was great meeting you, Kam. Nice seeing you again, Nicola. Colleen, hang in there, kid. 'Bye."

He was gone before anyone else had time to utter a single word.

" 'Hang in there, kid?' " Kamal repeated puzzlingly.

"It's an expression," Nicola explained. "Slang."

"Yes." Kamal was clearly perplexed. "But it does not seem like something a man would say to the woman he has been—"

"I'm awfully tired. I think I'll go to bed," Colleen said. She couldn't bear to listen to Kamal try to interpret Jack's glib dismissal.

"Colleen?" Nicola followed her to her room. "Are you okay? I—I'm really sorry—"

"Don't be." Colleen laid her hand on her friend's arm and gave it a sisterly squeeze. "I'm glad you came in when you did."

Nicola's lips curved into a teasing smile. "That's tactful of you, Colleen, but I don't believe it for a minute." Her dark eyes were glowing. "Colleen, isn't this incredible? Who could've dreamed it? We've been in Buffalo less than a week and we both found someone to fall in love with!"

"I'm not in love with Jack Blackledge!" Colleen cried vehemently.

"Colleen, I've known you for over five years. And in all that time this is the only time you've ever been so—uh—physical with a guy. And on the first date, too! Trust me, it must be love."

Six

"I'm not in love with Jack Blackledge," Colleen said aloud for at least the tenth time that morning. She'd fallen asleep mumbling it last night. Now, she was driving to work, trying to concentrate on the directional signs because she wasn't yet completely familiar with the route.

Nicola was wrong. It was generous of her friend to assume that something as noble as love had been governing her actions last night, but she wasn't in love with Jack Blackledge. She couldn't be! He was not the caring, sharing, easygoing, and open man she had always imagined for herself; he was moody and difficult, cynical and arrogant. She would never fall in love with a man like that. Would she?

And wasn't love based on honesty and trust? Well, she didn't dare be honest with him about her financial status because of his odious intent to marry for money. No woman in her right mind wanted a man who would value her bank balance more than her love.

So why had she been kissing him as if she were a woman lost in the throes of passion, allowing him to touch her, to evoke feelings in her that she'd never before experienced? Nicola had challenged her on that this morning as they both raced around the small apartment, trying to grab a bite of breakfast before leaving for work. And Colleen forced herself to face the shameful truth.

She wanted to go to bed with him. It was an electrifying admission for her to make to herself. She, Colleen Elizabeth Brady, quintessential good girl, was lusting for a man who made no pretense of loving her, who would have no qualms about using her and then dumping her. Or even worse, marrying her for her money—should he ever find out that she had it.

He wouldn't find out, Colleen vowed. She would not tell Jack that she had ties to one of the richest families in the country.

Furthermore, she would cure herself of this risky sexual attraction by staying as far away from him as possible. An infatuation needed the reinforcement of proximity, of continual exposure. She would try to keep away from her desk when he was at his, and she would avoid all after-work contact with him. She would build herself such a busy social life that she wouldn't have the time or energy to give a single thought to Jack Blackledge. Even if it meant asking Nicola to fix her up with blind dates who couldn't speak English.

But the effects of her pep talk fizzled when she arrived in the city room. Jack wasn't at his desk and, instead of relief, a fierce disappointment washed over her.

Kazorowski was at the coffee machine, and Colleen joined him there for a cup of the muddy brew, conveniently forgetting her own thermos filled with drinkable coffee at her desk. "Where's Jack?" she asked ever-so-casually.

"He's working at home today," said Kaz, grimacing between sips of thick, black coffee. "Has he, er, been working closely with you, showing you the ropes?"

Colleen knew that the managing editor was really asking if Jack had deigned to allow her to write a column yet. The answer to that, of course, was no. "I'm learning more every day," she replied. Her answer was as intentionally vague as his question had been.

Kazorowski got the message. He gave her a rueful smile. "Hang in there, kid," he said, and shuffled off.

She felt a hot flash of color suffuse her cheeks. That had been Jack's getaway line last night. She remembered how desperately eager he'd been to escape; the mere suggestion of sharing a quiet cup of coffee with her and her friends had sent him running. Because he didn't care about her at all, Colleen reminded herself bluntly. He made use of her company—and her body—only when it suited him.

The realization hurt. She might not be in love with him, but she was in deeper than she'd thought, and that was bad. Purposefully, defiantly, Colleen thrust Jack Blackledge from her mind and threw herself into a whirl of busywork.

First, she dug into the food department's files for requests and responses in preparation for the next two weeks' readers' recipe exchange. Then the entertainment editor asked her to update the obituaries of a number of television and film stars. Having obituaries prepared for people who were alive and well had always struck her as slightly ghoulish, although she could see the practicality for it. Still, spending hours writing about the living as if they were dead left her in a somewhat sepulchral mood.

She was delighted when Susan Farley and Christina Fusco, the two reporters who'd befriended her on her first day at the paper, invited her to join them for lunch at the Steak Escape. There, she feasted on a high-cholesterol, high-calorie cheese steak and all the fixings, without an iota of remorse. She returned to the newsroom refreshed and tackled her work with renewed optimism. Today recipes and obituaries, tomorrow original columns, she told her-

self. Maybe. If she lived long enough. . . . She had
to smile at her own dreadful pun.

"Looks like you're having fun. Care to share the
joke?"

Colleen's head whipped up at the sound of Jack's
voice. He was standing a few feet away, near his own
desk, watching her. She willed herself not to flush
or blush or otherwise appear affected by his presence. "Actually, I was getting ready to knock off for
the day," she said, shrugging. Her deliberately dif-
fident tone sharply contrasted to the riot going on
inside her. She glanced at her watch. "It's past two,
and I've been here since shortly after six this
morning."

She leaned forward and switched off the machine.
The rest of the obituaries could wait until tomorrow.
If a celebrity were to meet an untimely demise, she
hoped it would be one of those whose obits had been
newly updated.

"I was hoping I'd catch you before you left," Jack
said, moving closer.

Colleen permitted herself to steal a quick glance
at him. He was back in jeans, well worn blue ones,
and a yellow knit polo shirt. Tension and strength
were vibrating from him. She quickly looked away.
"Why?" she asked, and was pleased at the indifference, credibly feigned, in her voice.

Jack smile, a charming boyish smile that had
undoubtedly worked well for him in the past. Very
well. Even knowing that it was contrived, Colleen
felt its potency and had to fight to keep herself from
responding with a smile of her own.

She won the battle. "Why?" she repeated. Her face
expression deadpan.

Jack's smiled dimmed a little. "Well, it seems that
my mother and her sisters have suddenly developed
an overwhelming desire to take a boat ride on the
Maid of the Mist. Naturally, they want us to join
them and then have dinner together afterward."

Colleen eyed him coldly. So this was the way he

was going to play it. Complete denial. He was going to pretend that their passionate interlude yesterday had never happened, that they were simply coworkers on an assignment. "No," she said briskly. "Sorry, but I can't make it. You'll have to give my apologies to your mother and aunts."

"They're expecting to see you, Colleen. And we have an agreement, remember?"

"Yes. An agreement to deceive three nice ladies who don't deserve to be tricked. Count me out from now on, Jack."

She pointedly ignored him while she made a great production of straightening her desk and gathering her things together. But she was tautly aware that he was watching her every move.

He closed the gap between them with two giant strides. "Don't you trust yourself to spend time with me after what happened last night, Colleen?" he asked in a low, mocking voice.

Colleen's stomach lurched. Pretending that last night had never happened was infinitely preferable to having him acknowledge it so obnoxiously. Well, two could play that game. "Last night? Do you mean when you ran away from Nicola and Kamal and me as if we were harboring some fatal disease?"

"I guess it might've looked that way." Jack had the nerve to laugh. "But I was talking about what happened before I—"

"—took off like a rude, gutless clod?" she finished with acid sweetness.

"You've certainly changed your tune since dinner last night, when you described me as sensitive, sweet, thoughtful and—what else?—oh yes, gentle."

"I used up all my talent for fiction then. I don't have any more to spare."

"And even if you did, you wouldn't waste it on me?"

Her brown eyes flashed. "How true."

He moved a step closer, so they were only inches

apart, and she could feel the heat emanating from him. Her heart did a wild somersault.

"Let me get this straight: You're angry with me because I didn't extend our role-playing to include your roommate and her boyfriend." His onyx eyes glittered with challenge. "You wanted me to sit around and pretend that we're a couple, just like them. Maybe make some plans to double-date, exchange amusing little anecdotes about each other and our relationship. Stuff like that."

Put that way, it seemed ridiculous. *She* seemed ridiculous. Colleen fumed. "I'm angry with you because you're a self-admitted user who used me to placate your relatives and—and who wasn't above using me for a little sex, either."

"If I was using you, you were using me right back, honey. And enjoying yourself thoroughly in the process." He reached over to tuck a loose strand of hair behind her ear. She swatted his hand away.

"Don't even try to suggest that I—"

"—heated up like a torch when I kissed you?" Jack suggested silkily. "That's what really has you steamed, isn't it, Colleen? The fact that you were willing and ready to give up your much vaunted virginity to—"

"I was not!" she interjected fiercely. "I never would have—"

"Sweetie, if your friends had arrived a little later than they did, they would've found us in bed."

Enraged and humiliated, Colleen impulsively drew back her hand to slap him.

"Go ahead," Jack taunted. "Hit me. We already have an audience. Why not give them a full-blown melodrama to savor? We'll be starring in hot news-room gossip for weeks."

That horrifying prospect promptly restored her lost control. Colleen's hand slid to her side and she furtively glanced around her. An embarrassingly large number of staffers were staring at them with undisguised enthusiasm. Though they were out of earshot, just the sight of Black Jack and Colleen standing toe-to-toe, obviously engaged in an intense, angry conversation, was enough to spark their interest.

Colleen slowly backed away from Jack, schooling her features into what she hoped was an unreadable expression. She picked up her things.

"Show's over?" Jack asked, grinning broadly.

"You're a vain, arrogant—cockroach!" she hissed, wishing she could come up with something more effective.

"Cockroach?" Jack echoed. "Well, it's not as clichéd as rat or snake, but it still isn't all that clever. Can't you come up with a really original insult? You're supposed to be a writer."

"I haven't been doing much writing lately. In fact I haven't been doing any! I've been spending my time matching recipes with requests and suffering through unwatchable movies and updating obituaries instead of working on the columns I was hired to write."

She started to make her exit. Jack blocked her way. "Would you consider . . . collaborating with me on a column?" His gaze was intent.

Colleen tried to walk around him, but he skillfully matched her every step, keeping himself lodged firmly in front of her. "I have some ideas for several columns," he continued, never missing a beat. "But I could use some help with the content. How about it, Colleen? We'll have a brainstorming session and see what we come up with."

"You're trying to bribe me into going with you today. That's the only reason you're offering to—"

"But the point is, I *am* offering, Colleen. If you really want to write a column, you'll grab the chance and not fret over my motives."

She stared up at him warily. "You'll really let me write a column if I come with you and your family today?"

"If what you come up with is any good, if it's publishable, then we'll proceed from there."

Colleen thought about her fervid vow to keep away from Jack Blackledge and weighed it against the chance to write a column, which would entail her spending more time with him. She tried to ignore the excitement surging through her. This was a professional decision she was making, she told herself. Strictly professional. Viewed in that light, she would be crazy to turn down the first—and so far only—chance she'd been given to do a column.

"Can I trust you to keep your promise and give honest consideration to what I've written?" she asked sternly. "You won't go back on your word tomorrow, when you don't require me as a prop in your girlfriend game?"

There was a gleam in his eye. "Unlike you, I don't renege on a deal, Colleen."

"I don't—" she began hotly.

"You were about to do it today by refusing to come with me," he chimed in, cutting off her protest. "Our deal included you playing the part of my girlfriend until my mother and aunts left for Florida. We even shook on it, remember?"

Oh, she remembered. It had seemed easy and uncomplicated at the time. But now . . . Colleen dragged her gaze away from him. She wouldn't debate the issue, not now.

"Do I need to change clothes for the *Maid of the Mist*, or can I wear what I have on?" she asked stonily.

Jack's eyes swept over her sand-colored cotton jumpsuit. The jumpsuit enhanced every curve of her slender figure, and the round cloth buttons that extended from the hollow of her throat to below her navel tempted him to unfasten them one by one. He swallowed the lump in his throat. "What you have on is fine. Let's go."

Within an hour Jack, Colleen, and the three widowed sisters were aboard the *Maid of the Mist* as the boat edged close to the cascade of thundering waters that was Niagara Falls. Every passenger wore the provided thick rubber slicker, hat, and boots to protect them from the thick spray generated by the Falls.

"This is fun!" Colleen exclaimed as she hung on to the railing and gazed up at the mist-shrouded Falls.

"Better than a ride at Disney World?" Jack asked dryly.

"At least as good," she replied, ever loyal. "My sisters and my nieces and nephews are going to love it! I can't wait for them to visit."

"Be careful what you wish for," Jack cautioned. "You just may get it. Families have a way of appearing, you know."

Colleen laughed. "I'd love to have my family visit me—as long as they stay off the subject of prospective mates."

"Honey, you've summed up my sentiments exactly."

Colleen smiled broadly. She felt exhilarated and exuberant; her earlier gloom and irritation had completely evaporated. She knew why, of course—because she wasn't dealing with depressing obituaries, because she was finally going to get a chance to write a column. Her buoyant spirits were completely unrelated to being the focus of Jack's admiring attention.

Jack stood next to her at the railing, his arm draped loosely around her shoulders. His mother and aunts were sitting on one of the benches inside the boat. Though they were out of the older women's sight, Jack and Colleen kept the conversation flowing pleasantly between them. Neither mentioned that it was unnecessary to play the part of lovers out of range of their audience.

"What are all those people doing?" Colleen stared in astonishment at the figures on shore who were climbing a path almost leading under a small portion of the American Falls.

"That's the Cave of the Winds," explained Jack. "You don the rain gear and follow that wooden walkway up and under the Falls."

"Oh, I want to do it!" Colleen exclaimed.

"You get soaked, being so close to the water. And the raincoats and boots don't help much because they're already wet when you put them on."

"I don't care! Let's do it, Jack!" She smiled up at him, her eyes shining, her face alive with enthusiasm.

Jack felt a twinge deep in his gut. She was so young and vibrant and heartbreakingly lovely. And even in that ridiculous slicker and rain hat, she was sexy and tempting, her mouth soft and kissable, her big, beautiful eyes luminous. He felt a conflicting urge to ravish her and protect her at the same time, and the paradox left him emotionally sandbagged.

From the moment he'd run out of her apartment the night before, fleeing from the powerful emotions she had evoked in him, he'd thought of nothing but Colleen. When his mother suggested this *Maid of the Mist* boat trip, he hadn't answered with his usual sarcasm, but had leapt at the chance to spend additional time with Colleen. When she'd refused to accompany him, he'd been more disturbed than he cared to admit, thus his column bribe.

Which he intended to honor. Strangely enough, he no longer minded the prospect of having her as his apprentice, not even if her prose turned out to be unsalvageable. His attitude had undergone a 180-degree turn since she'd arrived at the *T-G*, but he didn't even question it.

"Excuse me, could you step aside for just a moment?" A portly middle-aged man with a video camera called out to Jack and Colleen.

They glanced around to see an elderly couple moving toward them, accompanied by a woman and two teenagers, a boy and a girl. All of them grinned and waved into the camera.

And then, the teenage boy boosted himself up to sit on the railing. "Hi, Dad!" he called, and began to wave vigorously. The family watched him, their grins in place. The father held the camera steady and kept filming.

Jack and Colleen exchanged glances of disbelief. "Jack, he could fall into the water," Colleen exclaimed at the same moment that Jack shouted to the boy, "Get down from there. Do you want to fall in and drown?"

A split second later, the boy lost his balance and started to topple backward. Colleen screamed. The father kept filming. With a professional athlete's timing and reflexes, Jack grabbed the boy's legs just as he started to go over the side. Within moments, two other passengers rushed over and helped him hoist the boy back onto the boat.

"You idiot!" Jack shouted at the boy, then turned to the father. "That was the stupidest stunt I've ever seen in my entire life. You—"

"You ruined our video," the boy's sister interjected crossly. "We were going to send it into *America's Family Videos* to be shown on TV. Mark was supposed to fall off the railing and into the water. Falling is hot and nobody's fallen off the *Maid of the Mist* yet. They would've picked it to be on the show for sure."

Colleen took one look at Jack's incensed, incredulous expression and quickly grabbed his arm and dragged him away. Two of the boat's crew members stepped in to deal with the prospective filmmakers.

"You're a hero, Jack!" she exclaimed, throwing her arms around him impulsively. "You moved so fast, you were as quick as lightning. You saved that boy from going over the side!"

"The whole idiotic family should be locked up on grounds of extreme stupidity," ranted Jack. "The water has a whirlpool effect—if that kid had fallen in, he would've been sucked right under."

He felt wired. The danger of the situation had called forth a burst of adrenaline, which pumped through his veins. There were studies proving that danger faced and overcome increased ardor and bolstered desire, but Jack wasn't thinking of social-science experiments. He only felt Colleen's arms around him. He quickly enfolded her in his embrace.

It seemed so natural and right to hold her. When she dropped her arms and attempted to move away, he tightened his grip, keeping her firmly against him. "They were willing to risk the kid's life in order to get their video on TV!" he exclaimed indignantly. "I'm surprised they didn't decide to send Junior over the Falls in a barrel and film that."

"Going over the Falls in a barrel has been done," Colleen pointed out dryly. "It might not be a sure pick for the show. Besides, falling is hot," she added in a dead-on imitation of the gum-chewing teenage girl.

Laughter rumbled in his chest. "It's not nice to make fun of moronic tourists who aspire to make their national television debut, Colleen." He lowered his head to hers until their foreheads were touching. "So you think I'm a hero, hm?" Having her view him in that light held surprising appeal for a man who claimed to revere his reputation as uncaring and coldhearted.

Colleen shivered, and not from the cool spray of the water. "You are," she said softly. "You didn't have to get involved, but you did. You chose to help that boy."

Her heart burgeoned with hope. Didn't this prove his mother and aunts were right? There was a caring, unselfish man behind the carefully constructed Black Jack facade.

Their mouths were so close that their breath mingled. "You were so brave and strong," she whispered.

"You're making too big a deal out of the whole thing, Colleen," Jack murmured. His lips brushed her mouth once, then lifted, then touched it again.

"It is a big deal." She stood on her toes and angled her head slightly. This time it was she who caressed his mouth with hers. "You may want to hang on to that tarnished image of yours, but I won't let you, not when it deserves to be polished."

Their eyes met and held for a long moment as awareness and desire burned through them. Silently, simultaneously, they both pressed closer.

"This is crazy," Jack growled as he slipped his hand under her thick curtain of hair to cup the nape of her neck. "We're on a damn tourist boat, for goodness' sake. There's five pounds of waterproof rubber between us." He frowned at the oversize slickers.

"Feels more like ten pounds," Colleen murmured, sliding her arms around his neck.

His fingers stroked the silken skin of her nape as he gazed down at her. "Not only that, we could be at the mercy of that lunatic with the video camera." He touched her lips with his thumb, tracing their shape. "Since the fall overboard didn't pan out, maybe he'll focus his television aspirations on us."

Her lips parted pliantly, responding to the sensuality of his touch. "Do you think we'd be interesting enough to be picked for the TV show?" It was difficult to keep up the repartee when all she wanted to do was close her eyes and melt into him. "If falling is what's hot—"

"Oh baby, what a lead-in." Jack laughed softly. "I can think of at least a half dozen lines, all having to do with what's hot." His lips played with hers. "And *who* is hot."

Colleen clung to him, her eyes heavy-lidded and dreamy. She felt hot, as if a wildfire were blazing inside her, setting her aflame with need, with desire. And she'd never before had the kind of wild and wanton thoughts that were tumbling through her mind at this moment. She wanted him to kiss her, *really* kiss her, the way he had last night, slow and deep and hard. She wanted to feel his hands on her, caressing her bare skin, touching her breasts, her nipples, between her thighs . . .

The boat lurched slightly, knocking them both off balance. Jack automatically grabbed the railing to steady himself, keeping one arm firmly around Colleen. She hung on to him, feeling a bit dazed and disoriented, as if she'd been thrust awake in the middle of a dream. A sexy, wonderful dream—and a shocking one.

She pressed her hands to her flushed cheeks as realization of time and place fully dawned. She hadn't given the boatload of tourists a thought! When she was in Jack's arms, it was as if they were the only two people in the world.

"I—I'm going down to find your mother and aunts," she said, drawing away from him.

Jack let her go. She looked as shaken and bemused as he felt.

So now he knew. He frowned thoughtfully. The profound urgency he had experienced last night as he'd kissed her had been no aberration. Nor had it been overblown by his feverish imagination. The same explosive passion and need had happened today, the moment he had taken her into his arms.

The question was, What was he going to do about it? There seemed to be only two options. One was to go the noble route and stay away from her. She was young, sweet, and innocent, the type for whom commitment had been invented. And he was none of those things. The kindest thing he could do would be to keep out of her life.

But then Black Jack was not known for his kindness. He took what he wanted. And he wanted Colleen Brady. Taking her to bed and quenching his desire for her was option number two. This struck him as far more appealing.

For one guilty moment he remembered her idealistic revelations about love and sex, but he quickly banished them from his mind. She was twenty-three years old; wasn't it time for her to trade in fantasy for the reality of passion? Of course it was, he assured himself righteously. He would even be doing her a favor of sorts, teaching her to recognize the difference between love and sexual infatuation so that when her own Mr. Right came along, she would know him.

He abruptly dropped that rationalization. There was something profoundly disturbing about the thought of Colleen and an imaginary Mr. Right. Being Jack, he refused to question why. Far better to contemplate the tantalizing prospect of Colleen in his bed and nothing beyond that.

It was decided, then. Turning on his most charming smile, he went off to find Colleen.

Seven

Colleen glanced at Jack in confusion as he swung
his car into the driveway of a white brick ranch-style
house. They'd left his mother and aunts at the hotel
after a sumptuous buffet dinner following their tour
of the Cave of the Winds. The older women hadn't
joined them for that, preferring to wait in a nearby
park. The two of them had had a riotous time climbing, then slipping and sliding up and down the path
alongside the Falls and getting soaked by the water
raining down on them as they held hands and
laughed like a pair of delighted tourists—or, perhaps, like a pair of lighthearted lovers.

Jack braked to a stop before pulling into the
garage a few feet in front of them. "I'm not going to
bother putting the car in the garage. I've been thinking about getting one of those electronic door openers for years, but I never seem to get around to it,
so the car usually stays here in the driveway."

A fine drizzle was beginning to fall outside, spot-
ting the windshield. Colleen turned to Jack.
"Exactly where are we?" she asked, though she was
fairly certain she knew.

"My place."

Was she imagining the challenging tone in his
voice? An unsettling combination of apprehension

and anticipation streaked through her. "You told your mom we couldn't spend the evening with them because you were tired. You said we'd had a busy day and you were going to take me home."

"I *was* tired. Tired of being observed by three adoring chaperons. And I meant home—to my house." He watched her nibble her lower lip as she squirmed in her seat, and he smiled. She was very aware of the implications of being alone with him. A good sign, a very good sign. "Since it's only eight o'clock, I thought we could get started working on the column," he added nonchalantly.

His place. Colleen sat stock-still and watched Jack walk around to her side of the car. The rain had started to pick up, and when he opened the door for her and offered her his hand, a splash of cold water blew inside. It struck her as ominous.

"Your mother and aunts aren't here to watch you play the role of gentleman suitor, Jack," she said. "You don't have to go through the motions just for me."

He smiled. "Maybe I want to, Colleen. And maybe I'm not merely going through the motions." When she didn't accept his proffered hand, he took hers and tugged gently. Automatically, she climbed out of the car.

He kept her hand tucked in his as he rushed her through the rain into the house, flicking on the lights as soon as they entered. "First, I'll give you the grand tour," he said lightly, taking her from room to room, keeping up a steady stream of comments, none of which required a response.

Which was fortunate, because Colleen gave none. Not when he showed her the large modern kitchen or the living room with its plush carpeting and wide L-shaped sofa and brick fireplace and the thick cushions arranged on the floor in front of it. Not when he led her in and out of his bedroom, which was decorated in shades of forest-green and gray and whose focal point was the king-size bed with its brass head- and footboard. Nor when he pointed out the sunken whirlpool tub in the mirrored bathroom.

She was still silent when they ended the tour in his den, with its wall-length bookshelves and state-of-the-art computer equipment. There were also a wide desk and upholstered chair, along with a black leather couch and small refrigerator. Rain pattered against the skylight.

"Can I get you something to drink?" Jack offered. "I have everything—soda, beer, wine, even wine cool-ers. Or maybe you'd prefer a hot drink. Coffee? Tea?"

"Nothing, thank you."

"How about one of those exotic fruit drinks with crushed ice and a little paper umbrella in it?"

Her eyes widened. "You can make one of those?"

"Well, minus the little umbrella. I used to work as a bartender in San Francisco during the off season when I was playing for the Giants. I can fix any drink—and invent new ones."

"I don't want anything. If we're here to work, we'd better get started."

"Yeah." Jack dropped onto the sofa. "Sure. You're right. Have a seat." He indicated the sofa cushion beside him.

Colleen chose to sit on the chair behind the desk. She cast a sidelong glance at him and found him watching her intently. In that moment, he rather reminded her of her sister Erin's family cat studying the fish swimming in their aquarium.

She cleared her throat. "I—like your house," she offered nervously.

"Thank you, Colleen." Once again, his tone was pure politeness and she might have been fooled had she not seen the wicked gleam lighting his dark eyes.

She frowned. "It's not at all what I expected," she continued, a little defiantly.

"And what were you expecting, Colleen? An X-rated bachelor pad decorated in high sin? Mirrors on the ceilings and—"

"From the way you talk about your financial state, I thought you'd be renting some hovel without furniture or electricity or indoor plumbing," she interrupted. "You're not broke. You have a nice, beautifully furnished house that has every modern convenience. Your ex-wife didn't spend all your money, not by a long shot."

Jack grinned and stood up, sauntering around the desk to where she was sitting. "No, Donna didn't spend everything. I bought this place and also socked away a few grand in savings."

"Did you live here with her?" Colleen asked curiously.

"Donna in Buffalo?" Jack laughed. But this time the bitterness that usually accompanied the mention of his ex-wife was noticeably absent. "No way. We lived in California while I played for the Giants. I moved back to Buffalo and bought this place after we broke up."

"And you started working immediately as a sportswriter and eventually got promoted to columnist." Colleen added what she knew of his history. "Now you're syndicated and making even more money. You have no need to marry a rich wife." The notion cheered her immensely.

"Honey, if—and it's a very big if—I ever decide to marry again, I fully intend to get something out of it beyond the usual fictitious promises to love, honor, and obey. Cash will do nicely. We'll live on the new Mrs. Blackledge's money while I bank my entire salary."

"Let me guess—you won't bank your salary in a joint account," snapped Colleen. "It'll be all yours, because what's yours is yours and what's hers is negotiable. And you'll do all the negotiating in your favor."

Jack nodded. "You've got it, honey," he said congenially.

Colleen made an exclamation of disgust and jumped to her feet. "That's the most mercenary, greedy, despicable—"

"Hey, calm down! Don't go getting all bent out of shape on behalf of the new Mrs. Blackledge." Jack was laughing. "She doesn't even exist. And if and when she ever happens on the scene, believe me, she won't be some naive little lollipop who marries me for true love. She'll have her own reasons."

The swine, Colleen thought furiously as she headed for the door. Jack caught her around the waist and swung her back against him, locking his arms around her. "Let me go!" she demanded.

He nuzzled her neck. "I would if I thought for one minute that you really wanted me to."

"I do!" She tried to pry his fingers loose, struggling all the while.

He laughed again. "Colleen, let's not play games. We both know why we're here."

"I can't speak for you, but I'm here to work on the column you promised me." She wriggled against him and went still as she felt the hard power of his arousal.

"That's what having you here does to me," he murmured, positioning her even more intimately into the cradle of his body. He pressed a kiss into the nape of her neck and smiled as he felt the small shiver ripple through her. "That's what being near you does to me. I want you, Colleen."

His teeth closed lightly around her earlobe at the same moment that his hands moved from her waist to cup her breasts through the soft cotton of her jumpsuit.

"Jack, no." Colleen's voice was husky and thick and she wondered vaguely why she was whispering. There was no one else around to overhear her. "I can't . . . I won't . . ."

"Yes," he said. "You can. And you will."

He sounded far more certain than she did, Colleen thought dizzily. And no wonder. Despite her faint attempts at protest, she was leaning back into him instead of pulling herself out of his grasp. And though she'd started to yank his hands away, she somehow found her hands covering his, pressing them against her while her head lolled back against his shoulder.

She had to stop this, of course. She knew that, but before she could utter a word, he deftly opened the first three buttons of her jumpsuit and slipped his hand inside. Colleen started violently at the feel of his fingers on her bare flesh. "Jack," she whispered hoarsely. She intended to tell him to stop, to let her go immediately, but somehow the words were never spoken.

"Sh, baby, it's all right." His voice was soothing and seductive, distracting her. He kissed her neck, soft biting little kisses that made her ache. And all the while his fingers kept moving, kneading her soft flesh until a tiny moan escaped from her lips.

"It feels good, doesn't it, sweetheart?" His tone was as arousing as his wicked fingers, which had located the front clasp of her lacy brassiere and easily unfastened it.

Colleen's head was spinning. Her eyelids felt heavy; it took a great effort to keep them open. The feel of his big, strong hands on her bare breasts was beyond anything she had ever experienced. He fondled her, cupping and caressing, and she felt her nipples growing tighter and more sensitive. She wanted him to touch them, wanted it with a desperation that shocked her.

"Jack, please!" She turned her head to protest, but Jack seemed to misinterpret her needy little cry.

"Yes, baby, yes." His mouth caught hers, his tongue slipping inside to rub hers as his fingertips touched her taut, sensitive nipples at last. He rubbed them, gently squeezing, until she was arching against his stroking hands and instinctively pressing herself against the thrusting strength of his arousal.

She lost the battle to keep her eyes open. She was so caught up in the new and delicious feelings enveloping her that she wasn't aware that while his right hand remained on her breast and continued to pleasure her, his left hand unbuttoned the jumpsuit all the way to her navel.

Colleen gasped when she felt his hard fingers on the soft, bare flesh of her belly. His thumb traced her navel, dipping into the hollow, and a streak of fire radiated from his fingertip to the secret core of her, which was moist and swollen and throbbing. She held her breath as his fingers inched toward the waistband of her bikini panties. Her entire body began to quiver.

And then he removed his hands from inside her clothing and scooped her up in his arms. The room seemed to tilt as he strode along, carrying her high against his chest. It was a jarring transition, from a mindless state of sensuous abstraction to one of action—purposeful, strong, and forceful action.

Colleen tensed. "What are you doing?" she asked in a jittery, high-pitched voice she scarcely recognized as her own.

Jack was too intent on his destination, the black leather sofa on the opposite side of the room, to note the anxiety in her voice. "Let's lie down, sweetie," he said huskily. "We'll be much more . . . comfortable that way." He deposited her on the sofa and lay down on top of her.

Colleen felt the full, hard weight of him upon her and a wave of panic assailed her. The passion that had melted her resistance earlier abruptly vanished and she was galvanized into some purposeful, strong, and forceful action of her own.

"Get off me!" She pushed him with both hands. "You're crushing me. I can't breathe!" Which wasn't exactly true. The voluptuous sensations of helplessness and breathlessness she was experiencing were alarmingly pleasurable, and if she had been drugged by passion, she would have luxuriated in them.

Even now, her judgment was beginning to cloud again. That horrified her. Colleen bucked and reared like a wild pony, pushing and struggling beneath him.

Jack braced himself on his elbows and stared down at her, his eyes cloudy, his expression dazed. "Baby, we—"

"I don't want this, Jack!" Colleen took advantage of his momentary weakness and slipped out from under him, landing on the floor with a thud. She quickly scrambled to her feet.

"Honey, of course you do." Jack levered himself to a sitting position. "I was going too fast and I scared you, that's all. Come here and I'll—"

"Take me home right now." Her voice quavered. She quickly rebuttoned her jumpsuit, her hands shaking. She didn't even try to fasten her bra. Its tiny clasp required a dexterity she knew she didn't possess at this moment, so it hung loose beneath her clothing, a reminder of their intimacy.

"What kind of game are you playing, Colleen?" Jack sighed impatiently. "One minute you're as hot as—"

"I'm not playing games!" she cried. Her face was crimson. "But you are, and I'm not in your league."

"Spare me the baseball metaphor!" Jack heaved a mock groan. "I've heard them all, I've made them all, from comparisons to the major and minor leagues to striking out to making it to each base. Well, you get the picture."

"Yes, I certainly do. You're making a joke out of— of—" Colleen paused. Was there a specific term to describe what had gone on between them? The rush of passion, the excitement and the fear, all the wild emotions . . . and he dismissed it as a joke! She felt a rush of tears blind her as she dashed toward the door.

"Colleen!" Jack bellowed after her. He rose shakily to his feet, his whole body throbbing with the force of his desire. He couldn't remember ever experiencing such burning, aching frustration. And he deserved it, a punctilious voice in his head intoned, for trying to seduce a marriage-minded, inexperienced young virgin.

He heard the kitchen door slam and knew she'd gone outside. Emitting a sound that was half sigh, half snarl, he followed and found her sitting in his car, her arms folded tightly in front of her chest, her face stormy as the night.

Jack pulled open the car door. "Come back inside, Colleen." The rain had escalated to a heavy downpour and he was getting soaked. "Now."

"No! I want to go home. Now," she added, perfectly mimicking the tone and inflection of his command.

"Colleen, don't you want to—uhhh—work on the column? Come back in the house and we'll—"

"How stupid do you think I am?" Colleen interrupted hotly. "I'm not about to fall for *that* again. You never intended to let me do a column at all—you only said so to get me to continue the charade for your family and to . . . to bring me here and try to get me into bed!"

She felt foolish and disillusioned. But most disturbing of all were her traitorous, instantaneous responses to him. Colleen trembled as she remembered how she'd let him touch her, how she'd wanted him to do so much more. . . .

She'd even managed to forget that his feelings for her went no deeper than physical desire, that she was no more special to him than any other woman he'd brought home for a quick romp in the sack. And from the gossip at work, she knew there had been plenty of those! He had no respect for her, not as a person, not even as a fellow writer.

He was a snake, all right, but an honest one, Colleen admitted grudgingly. Which made her a complete idiot, because she'd fallen for him anyway and couldn't even claim he'd deceived her with sweet words and promises of love.

"I don't want to stand out here in the rain and

get drenched while we argue, Colleen." Jack's tone was more coaxing now. "Come inside and we'll talk."

She was having none of it. "I'm not getting out of this car. If you don't want to stand in the rain, you'll have to get in and drive me home."

Jack growled an unintelligible curse and sloshed through the rain to the driver's side. "It would serve you right if I went back into the house and let you spend the night out here," he said. He inserted the key into the ignition and the motor roared to life.

"You're not doing me a favor by taking me home," Colleen retorted. "That's what you were supposed to do in the first place, but you—"

"Yeah, yeah, I committed the unpardonable sin of trying to make love to you. Well, let me tell you, baby, it didn't take much effort on my part, because you wanted it as badly as I did. I still do," he added with an injured air. "I ache from the back of my heels to the top of my head."

"Am I supposed to feel sorry for you? You're the one who—"

He didn't let her finish. "You're the one who put the brakes on after giving me every go-ahead sign a woman can give to a man."

Colleen blushed. Maybe what he said was true, but she wasn't going to compound her mistake by letting him put the blame for tonight's episode and its less than satisfying conclusion all upon her.

"Well, there was one sign you didn't give me, Jack—a sign that you care for me, that I'm something more than just another of your flings!"

Jack sighed. "You're talking like an overwrought virgin, Colleen. You surely don't intend to be one forever, do you? You're too passionate, too responsive, to live without love."

"I don't intend to live without love. But sex isn't love and—"

"Help! Stop! Not the love-and-sex lecture. Save your breath, honey. I already know it by heart."

"Then I have nothing more to say to you!"

"That's fine with me."

They didn't speak for the rest of the drive. When Jack pulled up in front of her apartment building, Colleen flung open the door before he had braked to a full stop. Jack caught her arm, restraining her, just as she was about to run out into the rain.

"Despite your atrocious behavior tonight, I'm not a man who goes back on his word," he said. His voice held a righteousness that further infuriated her.

"*My* atrocious behavior?" she spluttered. "If anyone behaved atrociously tonight, it was you, making a heavy pass when you know how I feel about—"

"I promised you a chance to do a column, and I'll honor that," he continued with maddening calm, totally ignoring her tirade. "Bring a sample to work tomorrow and I'll look it over. Good night, Colleen," he added dismissively, releasing her arm.

Colleen suppressed her roaring desire to launch a counteroffensive. Her passion had transformed itself into fury, and she wanted to fight with him as much as she'd wanted to make love with him just a short while earlier. But now, as then, her self-control exerted its power and restrained her. She stormed out of the car into the rain.

When she entered her apartment, she slammed the door behind her with such satisfying force that the sound echoed throughout the building. Nicola came running into the living room, and Colleen was about to initiate a spectacular diatribe when she noticed her friend's tear-streaked face and reddened eyes. "Nic, what's wrong?"

"Oh, Colleen, everything's wrong!" Nicola sobbed, sinking down onto the sofa. Colleen quickly hurried to her side. "Kamal's engaged, Colleen. I found out today. A nurse he used to date asked me if I knew about his fiancée in Aber—Ajer—"

"Azerbaijan," Colleen said. Nicola might not have paid attention to her relatives when they'd discussed the blood feud with the Armenian republic, but Colleen had.

"Whatever," Nicola wailed. "I thought she was just being spiteful—you know, the woman scorned and all, because Kamal was dating me now. She said there's this girl in a mountain village over there who's supposedly betrothed to him."

"Betrothed? That sounds medieval, Nic—the village girl from the old country who's brought over to be a bride in the new world. It can't be true."

"But it is, Colleen! I asked Kamal myself. He's been engaged to her for the past four or five years, and his aunt and uncle are going to send for her next year, when she turns eighteen. Then they'll be married."

"Why, she's just a child!" Colleen gasped. "And they've been engaged for years? It's medieval, all right, not to mention positively creepy!"

"Kamal has never even met her! Their relatives cooked up the entire arrangement and he went along with it. Willingly! He *wants* a young, backward bride from an Azer-something village. He thinks American women are too independent, too free-thinking, and too sexually forward."

"But he's not above using American women while waiting for his untouched bride to grow up!" Colleen's eyes flashed with indignation. "Oh, Nicola, I'm so sorry." She hugged her.

"Colleen, I've been such a fool! Kamal was willing to use me and the way I felt about him for a little extracurricular sex while all the time he's been engaged!" Nicola began to cry again. "We had plans to go away together this weekend, Colleen. To Toronto. It's only about an hour's drive from here, and Kamal wanted to show me the city."

"That's not all he wanted to show you," Colleen muttered darkly.

"I know. And if we'd gone, he would have found out that I'm not as sexually liberated as he thinks I am. Ironic, isn't it?"

"It stinks!" Colleen declared. She felt like crying, too. "Maybe we should've stayed in Houston or in Washington, Nic. Maybe our families are right, maybe we do need them around to keep tabs on us—and—and to fix us up with guys who wouldn't dare try to use us, because they'd have the Ramseys and the Shakarians to deal with if they did."

"Colleen, by the way you're talking I get the feeling that something happened with Jack tonight," Nicola said perceptively, temporarily shelving her own misery to focus on her friend. "Something not so good."

Colleen stared blindly ahead. "Jack doesn't have a fiancée tucked away, but he's perfectly willing to use me for—how did you put it?—a little extracurricular sex, even though he doesn't love me and doesn't even pretend to."

"Did you have a fight? Are you going to stop seeing him?"

"Yes, to both questions." Colleen gulped back the sob that rose in her throat. It was so stupid to cry over someone who didn't care, who didn't even want to care.

Nicola sighed unhappily. "Hard to believe that yesterday we were both happy and hopeful and in love and today we're dismal and depressed—and in love. I hate it, Colleen. Falling in love! Ugh! What an overrated experience. I guess I should be grateful that I never slept with Kamal. Can you imagine how terrible it would be to find out *after* you've made love with him that the man doesn't care and has been using you?"

It would be worse to know it before and do it anyway, Colleen thought gloomily. If she didn't start taking her own advice and avoid him, she could see herself going that route with Jack. She was especially at risk now, having sampled the yearning hunger and passion a man could evoke in a woman, thanks to Jack's expert tutelage. Well, yearning hunger and passion might be engrossing to read about, but they were too hurtful and confusing to live with.

From now on, there would be no more excuses, no more self-delusions.

The phone rang and Nicola sprang up to answer it. "For you, Colleen," she said wistfully.

Colleen's heart jumped. If it was Jack, calling to apologize or even to talk about what had happened tonight . . .

It wasn't. Rodd Garrett was on the line. They chatted pleasantly for a few minutes before Colleen told him that she couldn't go to the party with him next Friday because out-of-town friends were coming to visit. It was a lie, but a white one, sparing him the truth—that she just didn't feel like partying with anyone.

Rodd accepted her refusal gracefully and then asked if he could call her again. She said yes, and Jack's nasty innuendos seemed to echo in her ears.

"Rodd Garrett seems nice, and I'm not playing hard to get in order to trap him because he's a professional football player," she announced defensively to Nicola.

Nicola stared at her, baffled. "Did somebody say you were?"

"Jack did. He—" Colleen's voice trailed off. She was not going to talk about Jack Blackledge, she promised herself. She wasn't going to think about him either, and she informed Nicola of her vow.

"Good, because I'm not going to think or talk about Kamal anymore, either," Nicola said firmly. "And if we happen to forget, we can remind each other. We'll be our own support group. Near Victims of Men Who Use Women—like the sound of that?"

The two exchanged shaky grins.

"You've just given me the inspiration for a column, Nicola. Do you feel like collaborating with me for a while?"

"If it involves bashing men in general and Kamal and Jack in particular, sure," Nicola said with determined cheerfulness. "We'll simply postpone our ban on acknowledging their existence for another hour or so."

Colleen fetched a tablet and pen.

Jack reclined in the whirlpool, watching the rain pound against the skylight above him. A bolt of lightning flashed in the midnight sky and the rain escalated, sluicing down the glass in thick rivulets.

There was something primally soothing about lying in the warm, bubbling water while a storm raged outside. Jack felt the tension slowly seep from his body. He wished his mind would follow suit. Unfortunately, it did not. His thoughts continued to race through his head at rapid-fire speed.

All of them had to do with Colleen Brady. Images of her kept tumbling through his head: Colleen laughing as the spray from the Falls blew into her face on the Cave of the Winds walk, throwing her arms around him and calling him a hero on the boat, the stubborn determined set of her chin when she was mad at him, the way her velvety dark eyes softened when he took her into his arms . . .

His reverie segued naturally into what else happened when she was in his arms—her whole-hearted, impassioned responses, which she was too innocent to disguise, her whispery soft moans, the feel of her young mouth open and hungry under his. He imagined her with him here, now, and his blood heated.

He was no longer relaxed. Jack turned off the water and began to towel himself dry. His body throbbed with urgency. Tonight didn't have to end like this, he decided. Ever a man of action, he strode to the phone and impulsively dialed Colleen's number.

It wouldn't take much to get her back here, he assured himself; she wanted him as much as he wanted her. True, he'd been a bit brusque with her earlier, but he could remedy all that with some sweet talk. He would even drive over to her apartment and pick her up—that in itself was a big concession. Usually, the recipient of his late-night summons was required to provide her own transportation.

"Colleen doesn't want to talk to you," Nicola Shakarian's cool voice informed him moments later. "She refuses to come to the phone."

"What?" Jack was so taken aback, he nearly dropped the receiver. "Why?"

There was a momentary pause while Nicola passed along his question to Colleen. Then she was back with an icy, "She says you know why."

"Well, I don't!" Jack snapped, and hung up. But he did know. Colleen wasn't going to let him treat her like a casual fling. If he wanted her, he was going to have to go through the motions of acting like he was in love with her.

Part of him wanted to say the hell with it, to pick up the phone and call someone else, someone who would use him just as he was using her, and not care. Someone who would expect nothing of him— and give him nothing in return except the use of her body for a few hours. It was an effective way of satiating the body while numbing the mind.

Instead, he climbed into bed alone, scowling into the darkness and wondering why his remedy for forgetting Colleen held absolutely no appeal for him. Worrying why it didn't.

Sleep didn't come easily. The strangest thoughts kept popping, unsolicited, into his head. He found himself thinking that he was now, at thirty-three, the same age his father had been when he had been born. And his dad had always joked about what a late start he'd had as a father.

Late start? Jack sat up in bed. Good Lord, he was in his prime! He had plenty of years ahead to father a child, to be the strong and energetic head of a young, growing family. Just as his father had been.

He felt a lump form in his throat. His dad had been everything a father could be to a boy. Jack remembered the endless hours his father had devoted to him, helping him learn how to throw, catch, and hit a ball. They'd gone everywhere together—hunting, fishing, to ball games and car shows and Scout meetings. There had never been a prouder father than Bob Blackledge. He'd never missed a single one of his son's baseball games, from Little League right up to the major league.

Jack felt a fresh surge of hatred for the drunken driver whose car had jumped the guardrail and plowed into his father's car on a warm spring afternoon thirteen years ago. Losing his dad was the worst thing that had ever happened to him. He'd had only twenty years with his father, he'd wanted so many more.

For the first time Jack allowed himself to wonder what his life would have been like if his father had lived. One thing was certain—he never would have married Donna. His father wouldn't have liked her; Jack had always known that, but he hadn't let it matter. Perhaps he wouldn't have been as restless and reckless, either, had he not been mourning his father during those wild years in his early twenties. Maybe he wouldn't have been driving too fast that hot summer night in California, maybe his car wouldn't have skidded and flipped, maybe he wouldn't have sustained the injury that ended his baseball career.

But all those things *had* happened, making him the man he was today—a man sitting alone in the darkness ruminating about his past because a certain little blonde, who was different from anybody else he'd ever gone out with, wouldn't let him use her casually for a little quick, easy sex.

Jack's mouth curved into a reluctant smile. Colleen wouldn't let him dump on her in any way; she could stand up for herself and did. She forced him to relate to her as an equal. His smiled widened. His dad would have liked her a lot.

Eight

"Here's the sample column you asked for," Colleen said coolly, handing Jack the typewritten sheet the next morning. She'd come to work early, planning to be at her desk before Jack arrived. Apparently, he'd had the same idea. He was already there when she entered the city room.

Jack glanced at the column. "The title is 'Sex, Lies, and Men'?" He frowned at her, his face reddening slightly. "This is a family newspaper, remember?"

"Read it. It's not pornographic, just a few good old home truths organized and categorized. Not that I believe for one minute that you'll allow it to be published as a column in your hallowed space. You'll never use anything I write. You're not about to give anyone else the kind of breaks you've had." She opened the top drawer of her desk and began to dump the contents into a shopping bag she'd brought with her.

" 'Men expect sex as a payment for dating, and the more expensive the date, the more pressure will be applied to end the evening in bed,' " Jack read. He looked up from the paper to stare hard at Colleen. "Uh-oh."

"It's time I faced the fact that I'm not going to be

a columnist at the *T-G*, and I committed myself to joining the food and entertainment staff full-time," Colleen told him as she emptied the second drawer.

" 'Men want sex with no strings attached,' " Jack read on, his dark brows arched. " 'Men will lie to get what they want, especially when it happens to be sex.' "

"I have some new ideas for the readers' recipe-exchange column, and there's a glut of second-rate movies scheduled to open over the Thanksgiving and Christmas holidays, which really aren't so far away, just a few months." The words spilled from her mouth. She didn't even stop to breathe.

" 'Men use sex as a weapon,' " Jack continued. " 'Men are impossible to be around when a woman says no to sex.' " He stood up, the paper still in hand.

"And, of course, there's always the obituaries," Colleen went on brightly. "They've got to be kept right up to the minute—you never know when there'll be a call for one or which one it'll be. I'll have plenty to keep me busy. I'm *glad* I won't have to worry about coming up with an idea for a column every week or so." She picked up the shopping bag and flipped the strap of her purse over her shoulder. "Good-bye, Jack."

"Where the hell do you think you're going?" Jack demanded.

"To see Mr. Kazorowski. I'm going to ask to be moved upstairs to food and entertainment. With any luck, I might get a desk and chair from this century." She cast a baleful look at her dilapidated desk and ancient chair.

"So you're going to run away without giving me— or the men of Buffalo—a chance to challenge this sexist treatise? Or to issue one of our own?" Jack tossed the paper down onto his desk. "No, Colleen. I don't think so."

Once again he planted himself directly in front of her, blocking the aisle, just as he had the day before.

"Put your things back in your desk and type this column into your terminal, Miss Brady. We'll run it on Tuesday, and I'll write my rebuttal—the men's side—for Thursday. Then we'll wait for our readers to join in the battle. We ought to get at least another week's worth of columns by quoting the letters that are sure to pour in."

Colleen stared at him, nonplussed. She'd been so sure he would reject the column that she hadn't even given a thought to what she would do if he didn't. And removing herself from his proximity had made such sense when she'd planned it last night. But here, now . . . "I don't, I'm not—" she began, but he started walking toward her, forcing her to keep stepping backward unless she wanted him to close in on her.

Which she definitely didn't. Colleen dropped everything on top of her desk and warily circled around to the other side. Removing herself from his proximity still made sense, she decided with a nervous gulp. "I thought you'd hate this column."

"I wanted to. But it's well written. You have a light, witty style, even when you're dealing with scintillating subjects like sex, lies, and men. The readers are going to enjoy responding. You've certainly inspired me. I'm going to write Thursday's column right away."

He sat down in her chair, then stood up a moment later, frowning and rubbing his neck. "How's this for an opening statement? 'Women withhold sex to get what they want, whether it's a new dress or a new dishwasher or a weekend trip or a wedding ring.'"

"It's insulting and untrue," Colleen said shortly.

"But it grabs your attention, makes you think about whether you agree or disagree, and most important, it makes you want to read on to see what other outrageous opinions will be revealed. Just like the column you wrote, Colleen."

"But I didn't deliberately use that criteria when I

wrote that column," she felt obliged to confess. "Last night Nicola and I were—"

"Having a terrific time trashing me, I'm sure."

"Not only you," Colleen admitted. "Kamal Veli was included, along with every other man we'd ever heard anyone gripe about."

"Whew, a *Today's Woman* girl hit squad. Glad I was safely at home out of firing range. I know why I was in for it, but why Kamal? He seemed like such a nice, courtly chap."

"Nice and courtly? Ha! He has a seventeen-year-old fiancée in Azerbaijan!"

"I see. Well, here's another nugget for my column—'Women delude themselves into believing that having sex and making love are the same thing. And that wanting to have sex and being in love are also the same.' "

"Because men do everything they can to foster those delusions," Colleen retorted.

"I don't. But you want me anyway, Colleen. If you hadn't run off in a furious virginal panic last night, today we wouldn't be raging with frustration and arguing about sex instead of having it."

"That reminds me of another truism I forgot to include in the column—men think that everything can be solved with sex."

Jack grinned. "Sweetheart, everything can."

"Temporarily, maybe." Colleen sniffed. "*Very* temporarily. Oh, what's the use? We can't work together, Jack. It's impossible. I'm going to see Kazorowski and—"

"Sit down and get to work on that column," Jack ordered. "Meanwhile, I'm going to requisition you a new desk. And I'll make sure you get a new chair today. That thing you have now could've been used in the Spanish Inquisition when the torture rack was out of order."

He turned and strode through the newsroom, leaving a bemused and bewildered Colleen staring after him.

*   *   *

"Why don't things turn out the way you think they will?" she asked Nicola later that day as they ate take-out fried chicken for dinner. "Last night I was positive I would never work with Jack, and I'd resigned myself to moving permanently upstairs to food and entertainment. But today he's praising my writing and running all over the building to find me a new chair and desk. I just don't understand."

"Sometimes things do turn out exactly the way you think they will," Nicola said gloomily. "Like today at the hospital. Kamal and I ignored each other except when it had to do with care of the children. And I heard he's already seeing someone in the X ray department. She probably couldn't care less that he's engaged. Oh, Colleen, I wish I could hate him, but I can't. And I just can't stop thinking about him and what could have been, either." She put down her chicken leg and began to weep.

Colleen was comforting her when the doorbell sounded. Nicola clutched Colleen's hand. "Do you think it could be him?" she whispered, and there was such hope in her dark eyes that Colleen fervently hoped it was. She rushed to fling open the door, willing Kamal Veli to be waiting there.

Jack Blackledge was lounging against the doorjamb. "You really should look before you open your door, Colleen. Even glorious Buffalo has a crime rate." He smiled a warm, sexy smile that could have melted her bones.

"What are you doing here?" Her voice came out in a nervous squeak.

"Have you had dessert?" He answered her question with one of his own. And then answered it. "Well, you're about to have the Jackson sisters' famous baked alaska. Jackson was my mother's maiden name, which, in case you haven't worked it out, is how I happened to acquire Jackson as a first name. Mom and the aunts are flying back to Florida in the morning, and they want to treat you to their special dessert before they leave. They're waiting for you at my house."

Colleen was immobilized by the conflicting emotions rushing through her. Anger, excitement, anxiety, and embarrassment each took a turn at the fore. Finally, she rallied herself to speak. "Jack, I'm not going to your house with you."

"Because you think this is a trap I've engineered to get you back to my place and resume my wicked seduction?" His dark eyes gleamed. "Believe me, we will not be alone at home. Mom, Aunt Judy, Aunt Dorothy, and their abominable concoction are firmly entrenched there."

"Baked alaska isn't abominable," Colleen protested. "I've only had it a couple of times, but it was very good."

"I'm glad you like it, you can have my share. Maybe you can even offer to print the recipe in the T-G's readers' recipe exchange. Make it truly a night of dreams for Mom and the aunts."

She should tell him to leave immediately; she should uphold her pledge to stay away from him. What she should *not* do was stand here, her lips curving into the grin she was trying so hard to suppress. Colleen knew all that yet she remained where she was. And didn't order him to go.

"I have to stay with Nicola," she hedged. "She's very upset and I don't want to leave her alone."

Jack shrugged. "Bring her along. The more the merrier . . . and the less I'll have to eat of that culinary catastrophe."

"She probably won't want to go . . ."

"Well then, we'll just have to talk her into it, won't we, Colleen?" He stepped inside the apartment, a relentless smile on his face.

Less than ten minutes later, Nicola, Colleen, and Jack left the apartment together. "I wish you'd've given us time to change," Colleen fretted, glancing down at her jeans and Houston Oilers sweatshirt.

"Well, the team is all wrong, but the clothes are fine," Jack replied dryly. "You don't have to dress up to impress my family, Colleen. They're permanently enamored of you. Mom is already wondering if the wedding will take place in Houston or Buffalo, and she's looking forward to meeting your folks."

"Colleen doesn't have folks, not if you mean parents," piped up Nicola, who was squeezed in the back. "She's got sisters, lots of them. And brothers-in-law and adorable nieces and nephews. But no mother and dad."

"You're an orphan?" Jack was astonished.

Colleen shrugged. "I guess I am, technically. My mother died of pneumonia when I was eleven. My father deserted our family when I was just a baby, and we've never heard from him since."

"Who took care of you after your mother's death?" Jack asked, shocked by the revelation. The thought of a small, orphaned Colleen stirred him.

He knew all too well the pain and confusion of losing a parent and the devastating effect it could have on one too immature to accept it. Colleen had been so much younger than he when she had suffered her own loss, and she'd also had to cope with an earlier abandonment.

He frowned. So it was no coincidence, no accident, that Colleen had shied away from a relationship serious enough to involve sex, just as it was no accident or coincidence that his relationships were based entirely on superficial sex, which could be equally distancing. They both had built self-protective walls around themselves, and their motives for doing so were oddly similar.

Yet here they were together. Though they'd fought the attraction, though they'd attempted to stay apart, somehow, someway, they kept coming together. Jack cast a quick glance at Colleen. It was as if only he could break through to the passionate young woman locked inside herself, as if only she could reach the lonely man who lived within him.

Jack shook his head. He was unused to such flashes of insight. They unnerved him.

"Her oldest sister, Shavonne, was only eighteen at the time." Nicola was chattering on, as familiar with the Brady history as Colleen was with the Shakarians. "It's a real-life Cinderella story! All the sisters—except Colleen, of course—married into the Ra—"

"Jack already knows my four sisters married four brothers," Colleen interrupted quickly. She was going to have to warn Nicola to keep the secret of the Ramsey wealth from Jack. "I bored him with the story the very first day we met."

"Within the first twenty minutes," Jack amended, then reached over to cover her knee with his hand. "But you didn't bore me, Colleen. I don't think you ever could."

"I drive you crazy instead," Colleen said lightly, removing his hand from her knee. It couldn't have been tenderness she'd heard in his voice; that wasn't his style.

She changed the subject.

The three widows were delighted to see them and handed each one a heaping plate of baked alaska. "We're so glad both you girls came." Jack's mother beamed. "It's lovely meeting Colleen's roommate."

"Your son is very persuasive," Nicola said, her dark eyes fixed thoughtfully on Jack and Colleen, who were sitting in a big, cushioned armchair in a far corner of the room.

An understatement to be sure, Colleen thought, gazing dizzily at Jack. She was on his lap; the moment they'd entered the living room he had pulled her down on him, fastening his arms firmly around her waist. With his hands thus occupied, he was unable to eat any baked alaska, and she wondered if that was his plan, given his lack of enthusiasm for the gooey, sweet ice-cream-and-meringue dessert.

But he kept her on his lap long after the plates

were cleared, holding her there during the entire two-hour visit. His hands were never still, but under the three older women's smiling scrutiny, his caresses were gentlemanly and respectably affectionate.

Then Nicola spilled her sad story about Kamal's old-world fiancée, and the three sisters were immediately caught up in it, offering consolation and advice, thereby ignoring Jack and Colleen. He took full advantage and proceeded to sneak a few scandalously intimate feels and murmur low, sexy asides in her ear.

Colleen grabbed both his hands in hers and held them fast. "What are you trying to do?" she said in an agitated whisper.

"Isn't it obvious?" he drawled. "I'm trying to turn you on. I thought even someone with your relative inexperience would've picked up on that."

"Jack, for heaven's sakes, your mother—"

"—is enthralled with Nicola's tale of woe. She isn't paying the slightest attention to us, and neither are my aunts. You see, now that they think we're a tried-and-true couple, they're ready to focus on someone else's life." His mouth brushed hers audaciously. "Kiss me, Colleen."

She ducked her head. "Are you crazy?" She wriggled on his lap in an attempt to break free.

He groaned softly but held her tightly in place. "I'm beginning to think I am. Keep still, Colleen, or you'll have to answer to the consequences."

Her cheeks turned a warm, rosy pink. "Jack, we've carried our charade far enough. Tomorrow your mother and aunts will be gone and this pretense will be over."

"I've been thinking about that." His voice was a deep, husky whisper that sent tiny arrows darting along her spine. When his big hand slid possessively along the length of her back, she reflexively arched into it, like a cat being stroked. "It doesn't have to be a pretense, Colleen. I don't think I want it to be."

She went still. "What do you mean?"

"I mean I'm attracted to you. You surely should know that by now. I—" He paused and cleared his throat. "I like having you around. I don't want to stop seeing you when they leave."

Her heart seemed to stop and then start again with a pounding thud. "Is this another ploy to get me into bed?" Her dark eyes flashed.

"If you mean do I still want to go to bed with you, the answer is definitely yes." He smiled lazily. "Would you prefer it if I told you I wanted to have a brother-sister relationship or just be friends?"

Colleen was mortified at the thought. "You said you like having me around," she said slowly. Her mouth was so dry, she had to swallow, hard. "Does that mean your sole purpose for seeing me wouldn't be . . . strictly sexual?"

His grin was positively treacherous. "What do you think, baby?"

"I think . . ." Her gaze darted to Nicola, who was crying again. The three sisters hovered over her, offering tissues. "I think that what I wrote in that column is true—that men will lie to get what they want, especially if it happens to be sex."

Instead of being offended, Jack laughed lustily. "We really are going to have a good time together, Colleen." He nuzzled her neck and regarded her through sexy, half-closed eyes. "That's a promise, sweetheart." He rubbed his thumb back and forth across her lower lip.

She'd also written about sex and promises in the column, Colleen recalled hazily. Something along the lines of all lies being promises or all promises being lies. She couldn't remember exactly, but right now it didn't seem to matter all that much, even though Jack was much too close and much too inviting, even though she was far too susceptible to his cocky charm.

She could recite all the very sensible and safe reasons why she shouldn't get involved with Jack

Blackledge, but suddenly they didn't seem to matter very much. She'd played it safe and sensible her whole life. Even her one stab at rebellion—refusing to settle down in Houston with a man of her family's choice—had not been impulsive and risky but controlled and carefully planned. Now she had her job, her apartment, her modest budget and lifestyle far, far below her means. What she didn't have was excitement or exhilaration . . . or love.

"Why the frown?" Jack murmured, shifting her on his lap so his mouth was even closer to hers. He nibbled on her lips and felt a hot longing and excitement shoot through him. He'd forgotten just how pleasurable anticipation could be.

"I was just thinking—" she began, but he quickly cut her off, placing two fingers on her lips.

"No, don't think, honey. Your problem is that you think too much. It's time to let yourself go with the way you feel. Loosen up. Lighten up."

She carefully removed his hand from her mouth. "I'm beginning to agree. That's what I was thinking about—how dull I am, how staid. How I've always walked the proper path, said the right things, done the right things. It's like I'm twenty-three going on sixty." And a repressed sixty at that! Her frown deepened.

"I understand perfectly, sweetie. Luckily, you're with the right person at the right time. I'll provide all the fun, adventure, and sex that's been missing from your life."

She regarded him archly. "What I'm looking for is the fun and adventure of a deep emotional involvement and sex with commitment."

His expression turned comically grotesque. "In that case—sorry, babe. I think you've got the wrong address."

They looked at each other and dissolved into laughter.

"I don't think so, Jack," Colleen said. Boldly, she ran her knuckles along the hard lines of his

jaw. *You've given yourself away, Black Jack.
You know exactly the way I feel about being in
love before making love, but you're still here.
You're as ready and willing to fall in love as I
am. It won't be long . . .*

"That must mean you're willing to play by my
rules, Colleen." Jack's tone was half teasing, half
challenging. *Timing is everything and my timing is
perfect. You're as eager to come to my bed as I am
to have you there. It won't be long . . .*

They exchanged satisfied smiles, their eyes glowing with their own secret triumphs.

The anticipation of making love to Colleen was so
pleasurable that Jack decided not to rush her into
bed. Paradoxically, since he was certain he could
take her whenever he chose, he was willing to give
her time so that she would think going to bed with
him was her own idea. He congratulated himself on
his cleverness and permitted himself to enjoy their
growing friendship with its enticing sexual over-
tones.

To Colleen it was a courtship. To be sure, not a
conventional one with candy and flowers, candlelight dinners for two, and evenings at the theater.
Sports-minded Jack had tickets to all the Buffalo
Bills games, liked to watch football and baseball on
television, and only went to movies that featured
antiheroes and lots of action.

Colleen didn't mind. She became an avid Bills' fan
and was relieved when the football strike lasted only
two weeks. While Jack cheered for his teams on TV,
she sat beside him reading or working on her
counted cross stitch embroidery or sometimes even
watching the game. And his action-adventure movies were so superior to the awful films she was
assigned to review for the *Times-Gazette* that she
came to appreciate them in a whole new way.

When Jack wasn't watching sports, he was playing them. Often, he dragged Colleen and Nicola to mixed-doubles tennis matches and volleyball games with his like-minded friends. He coached Colleen in preparation for the *T-G*'s softball team the next spring; they rode bikes. Colleen, who'd never been particularly physically active, was amazed at how much fun she was having.

They were physical in other ways, too. Jack found lots of reasons to instigate wrestling matches, which Colleen invariably lost and which inevitably ended up in hot kisses and caresses that treaded the fine line between light and heavy petting. Each time Colleen called a halt, but it became easier and easier to envision herself just letting go and giving in completely to the intense, voluptuous sensations aroused by his touch.

Jack didn't try to pressure her into bed, and his lack of coercion led to her confidence and trust in him. She remembered her theory about falling in love with a man who loved her—how he wouldn't view her as an outdated relic for not hopping into bed with him, but would respect her need to wait until she was sure, until the time was right. Wasn't Jack doing exactly that?

September melted into October. The weather turned cold as the wind from nearby Lake Erie gusted across the city in chilling blasts. At the *Times-Gazette*, everybody began to predict the arrival of the first snowstorm and to make bets as to how many feet of snow would fall. Colleen, who hadn't seen snow since moving to Texas seven years ago and who thought of snow in inches—never in feet and never in October—braced herself for her first infamous Buffalo winter.

She and Jack were together every day, in and out of the city room. Jack let her write a column once every other week, opening with a few comments of his own, then turning over the space to her with full writing credits .

"You're gaining a local following," Jack remarked

one morning as a pile of letters was delivered to Colleen's desk. He was filled with pride at the thought. Though he was usually intensely competitive, Colleen's reception by the *T-G*'s readers genuinely pleased him. "I think it's time you started doing one column a week. Say, every Tuesday?"

Colleen's face lit up. "That would be terrific, Jack. I already know what I want to write next."

He smiled. "Tell me."

She leaned forward and so did he, but their desks put a prohibitive distance between them. The newsroom was so noisy, she would practically have to shout to be heard. She had no other choice but to walk over to him to deliver her message. Colleen stood beside his chair, aching the way she always did when she was close to him. She'd become so addicted to that sweet, throbbing ache that it was difficult not to be near him. And when she was near him, she wanted—needed!—to touch him . . .

Their eyes met—hers, soft velvet brown, and his, sharp gleaming ebony.

"Sit on my lap," Jack said, his smile both tantalizing and challenging.

She wanted to. Sheer willpower kept her on her feet. "If I did, we'd become instant stars of hot newsroom gossip," she reminded him.

"I think we already are. Damn, this is when it would be convenient to have a private office, where we could—"

"Like Kazorowski's office?" Colleen feigned horror.

They both laughed because Kaz's dingy, cluttered office was hardly conducive to trysts.

"I thought I'd write a column made up of funny raps about the presidential candidates," Colleen said, and Jack was amazed at how easily they moved from charged sexual electricity to tension-relieving laughter to business. It was why they were able to work and play together so effectively, he realized.

"Though the election isn't until next year, the candidates seem to be climbing out of the woodwork,"

Colleen continued. "Since President Lipton can't run again, it's a wide open field."

"Losing the Lipton family is a real blow to all columnists," Jack said with an exaggeratedly doeful air. "They've been terrific fodder for both terms and I don't see their equals anywhere on the horizon. Remember when Lucas Lipton eloped last year with *Penthouse*'s Pet of the Decade? Ah, the mileage we got out of that one! The images of voluptuous, delectable Laynie Lynn in the Lincoln bedroom meeting the ghost of old Abe, of the Secret Service agents slavering over centerfolds of the babe—er—presidential daughter-in-law they're assigned to protect."

"Those were the days," Colleen said dryly.

"But I like your rap idea, Colleen. Hey, would you mind if your mentor steals it?"

"Try it and I won't let you win at wrestling tonight," she said, feigning menace.

He smiled rakishly. "Sweetie, when I wrestle with you, I win even if I lose."

They fell into the habit of having dinner together almost every night, at Jack's house, at Colleen's apartment, or at one of the city's many restaurants. Nicola often joined them. Since none of them was particularly fond of cooking, they ate a lot of takeout. Occasionally, Colleen would attempt an intriguing but easy recipe from the readers' recipe exchange; sometimes it was actually edible.

One night in early November, the three of them were dining on Buffalo chicken wings and salad at Harry's Sports Bar when a group of walking monoliths entered. An excited buzz swept the bar, drowning out the sound of the giant-screen television set that was broadcasting *Monday Night Football*. A number of patrons eagerly approached the newcomers.

"Those are a few of the Bills' defensive linemen," Jack remarked, "and hey, there's someone with them that I could fix you up with, Nicola. Rodd Garrett. He's a second-string offensive player and hasn't done much this year, but I've known him for a long time and—"

"Rodd Garrett?" Nicola repeated quizzically. "Isn't that the one who calls you sometimes, Colleen?"

Colleen nodded. Jack's jaw dropped. "Rodd Garrett has been calling you?" It was more of an accusation than a question. "Since when? And why?"

"He's called about every other week or so since I met him that night at Niagara Falls," Colleen said with a shrug. "We talk for a while and—"

"Has he ever asked you out?" Jack demanded. *Stupid question,* he berated himself. Of course Garrett had asked her out. Colleen was beautiful, sweet, sexy, fun to be with. What man wouldn't want to go out with her?

He didn't give her time to answer. "Have you ever gone out with him?" he pressed instead. A sickening surge of jealousy swept through him at the very thought of another man taking her anywhere.

Colleen shook her head. "You know I haven't," she said calmly. "I spend most of my time with you."

"Most, but not all," Jack snapped. He realized that he was being unreasonable, but he couldn't help it. "And if I didn't know Garrett was calling you, it's a very real possibility that I might not know you'd been seeing him on the sly."

"Well, I haven't been," Colleen snapped right back. "He calls me sometimes, we talk, he asks me out, and I say no because I don't want to go. I'd have every right to go if I wanted to, though," she added with a glare. "And it wouldn't be on the sly, either. We've never said one word about not dating other people."

"Oh boy, here it comes!" Jack growled. "The limits and the bounds every woman wants to set on a man she's dated more than twice."

"It seems to me like *you're* the one who wants to set limits and bounds," Colleen pointed out coolly.

"You're the one having conniptions about me dating someone else."

Jack's face turned brick-red. He turned to face Colleen, his black eyes smoldering.

"Which one is Rodd Garrett?" Nicola interjected in an attempt to defuse the brewing argument.

"The oversize hulk who looks like he drank steroids instead of milk at his mother's breast," Jack snarled.

"They all look like that," observed Nicola.

"Why don't you point out your admirer, Colleen?" Jack asked in the nasty mocking tone she hadn't heard him use for some time. It was hard to believe that she'd once been able to shrug off that tone of his. Now it wounded her, and the pain was razor-sharp.

"Never mind," Nicola said quickly. "I don't want to go out with any of those guys. They're too big. It would be like dating a wall. And Kamal says that size and aggression can be—"

"Kamal?" Colleen interrupted, grateful for the excuse to change the subject. She didn't want to argue with Jack in front of Nicola; she didn't want to argue with Jack at all. Unlike in the early days of their relationship, when they'd quarrelled all the time, they'd been so compatible for the past weeks that arguments between them were rare. In fact, the thought of him being furious with her made her eyes fill with tears. Colleen determinedly blinked them away.

"Are you talking to Kamal again, Nic?" she asked, turning away from Jack and concentrating fully on her friend.

"We started having lunch together again about three weeks ago," Nicola admitted. "We talk, we joke around together. We've always gotten along great. We're friends, that's all."

"Ha! Don't you believe it!" Jack inserted himself into the conversation. "A man and a woman can't

be friends. They're kidding themselves if they think
so. Everybody knows that."

"I don't—" Colleen began.

"Everybody but Colleen Brady knows that," Jack
cut in caustically.

Nicola glanced at her watch. "Would either of you
mind if we left now? My cousin Dana is supposed
to call with the plans for our grandparents' wedding
anniversary party, and I'd hate to miss her call."

The three of them rose and trooped out to Jack's
car. It was windy and cold and snow flurries whirled
around them. During the ride home, the flurries
changed their consistency, becoming big dry flakes
that fell faster and heavier. Colleen and Nicola discussed stiltedly the unforecasted snow, uncomfortably aware of Jack seething silently behind the
wheel.

Colleen hardly knew what she was saying to
Nicola. She couldn't keep her mind—or her eyes—
from Jack, who was so grim and unsmiling and
furious with her. *Because she'd talked on the
phone to Rodd Garrett?* And here she sat feeling sad
and intimidated, wondering what he would do when
they arrived at her apartment, trying to think of a
way to smooth things over, wanting to burst into
tears and beg him not to be angry with her.

The entire situation suddenly struck her as
grossly unfair. *He* was the one who'd behaved badly,
but she was the one worrying about placating him.
She'd watched her sisters in similar scenes with
their spouses, Colleen recalled, and it seemed to her
that it was always the Bradys who ended up doing
the conciliating and the mollifying. There had been
plenty of times she'd silently urged her sisters to tell
their men to take a flying leap, to make *them* do a
little peace making.

Well, here was her chance to take a stand and cast
off the Brady pacifism.

Nine

"You can just drop Nicola and me off in front of the building," Colleen said coolly as they neared their destination. "No need to bother parking the car."

Or coming inside. Jack added to himself. He cast a sharp glance at Colleen. Her arms were folded in front of her chest and her expression was mutinous. She was a far cry from the tearful, guilty penitent who'd gotten into the car with him.

He frowned, not at all pleased with the change. "And then what? Having served as your chauffeur, I'm just supposed to get lost?"

"You can go wherever you want," Colleen retorted. "But first, I think you owe Nicola an apology. Your temper tantrum in the restaurant made her very uncomfortable. That's why she wanted to leave."

"She wanted to leave the restaurant because she's expecting a phone call from her cousin Dana," Jack snapped.

"She was using that as an excuse," countered Colleen. "Dana called her yesterday."

"Could I officially withdraw myself from this fight?" Nicola asked dryly. "Jack, thanks for the ride, and you don't have to apologize because you didn't make me all that uncomfortable. I wanted to

133

get home because I really am expecting a phone call. Not from Dana, though. She did call me yesterday."

Colleen was temporarily diverted from her argument with Jack. "Nicola, are you expecting a call from Kamal?" she demanded.

Nicola gave a quick nod and hopped out of the car. "Carry on without me, you two. 'Bye."

Colleen was about to follow her, but Jack caught her arm and held her back. "We were in the middle of an argument, if you'll recall." But his voice had lost its caustic edge and his face was enigmatic, not angry.

"Sorry, but I can't stay and fight with you. I have to intercept that call. Nicola is going to be badly hurt if she lets Kamal hoodwink her into believing she stands a chance with him."

"Maybe she does stand a chance with him." Jack shrugged. "Azerbaijan is awfully far away, and she's right here in Buffalo. But it's none of your business either way, Colleen. Let Nicola handle her own love life, and concentrate on your own."

"My own *love life,* such as it is, is currently—"

He didn't let her finish. "Such as it is?" he repeated. Still holding on to her arm, he cupped her chin with his other hand and tilted her head back, forcing her to look directly into his glittering ebony gaze. "Would you mind explaining that?"

"What's to explain?" Colleen purposefully extricated herself from his grasp and was successful only because he chose to let her go. They were both fully aware of that. The wind howled outside, blowing a thick swirl of snowflakes against the windshield. Colleen shivered and pulled her coat more tightly around her. "I'd better go in so you can go home. The roads might get bad and—"

"The roads *will* get bad, I guarantee it." Jack started the engine. "But we'll be at my place long before they do." He swiftly steered the car into the street, ignoring Colleen's demands to be let out.

"That crack about your love life was a challenge if

I ever heard one," he said coolly. "You threw down the gauntlet, and ignoring it would mean I'm either indifferent or a complete wimp. I'm neither, Colleen."

Colleen fiddled with the clasp of her purse. "I don't know what you're talking about."

"Then I'll have to enlighten you, won't I? When a woman says *'love life, such as it is'* in a certain tone of voice, the natural assumption is that she doesn't have one worth talking about. Since I'm the only man in your life, I naturally take exception to that."

"The only man? You mean you don't believe I'm running around with Rodd Garrett on the sly?" Her anger had dissipated and a bubbling excitement was beginning to churn through her.

"Don't try to change the subject, Colleen. We're talking about—"

"Yes, I know. My love life." They'd come to a stop sign, and Jack glanced assessingly at her. She gazed at him with wide eyes. "Such as it is."

His black eyes narrowed to slits. It took him several long moments to begin driving again, even though there were no other motorists in the intersection. "I should have taken you to bed weeks ago," he said through gritted teeth. "I could have, you know."

"Is that so?" she asked cockily.

"Absolutely. You wouldn't have stopped me—you couldn't have."

She smiled sweetly. "Let's agree to disagree on that, Jack."

"I've created a shrew," Jack complained. "This is what I get for not keeping you satiated and compliant with sex. Well, I deserve it for not pressuring you, not rushing you, for giving you time to—" He broke off, his jaw rigid, his hands tightly clenching the steering wheel.

"Fall in love with you?" Colleen guessed softly.

A charged silence filled the car. And then: "I've never seen the roads get this bad so quickly." Jack's voice was brusque. "They're terrible. I really have to concentrate on driving."

An effective conversation stopper if there ever was one, Colleen thought grimly. She stared out the window. The roads were not all that bad, at least not yet. And she couldn't stop now. "Because I have, you know, Jack," she said quietly. "Fallen in love with you."

Simply saying it was a release, and a surge of joyousness flooded her heart as her body quickened with desire. It was all so natural and wonderful and right. She loved Jack, and her love enhanced and intensified the physical desire she felt for him. Loving him made the passion he aroused within her meaningful and profound, adding emotion and depth to the chemistry that had smoldered between them from the first day they'd met. There could be no shame in her wanting him, needing him, as she did.

"I love you, Jack," she whispered, savoring the sound of it. She'd been waiting her whole life to say those words to the man she loved.

Jack glanced at her covertly, his dark eyes thoughtful. He'd heard declarations of love before: from Donna, who had actually loved his pro ball career and what it could bring her, and from various others who'd wanted to manipulate him.

But his cynicism melted at the sound of those words on Colleen's lips. He knew she meant them. She hadn't uttered them while in the throes of sexual heat when "I love you" can be easily confused with "I love having sex with you."

It occurred to him that the time they'd spent together getting to know each other—letting her see him at his warm and thoughtful best as well as his irritable, impatient worst—had eliminated the possibility of her mistaking sexual infatuation for real love. Had he subconsciously sought that assurance? He was thunderstruck by the notion.

"Jack?" Colleen's voice held a sudden, anxious

note. "Say something, say anything. You've been sitting there silent as a stone since I"—she gulped—"since I told you I love you." A nasty prick of self-doubt made her flinch. What if he was aghast at her confession? Suppose he considered her avowal of love a burden instead of a gift?

Jack pulled the car into his driveway, right up to the garage door. "It seems incredibly prosaic at a time like this, but I have to get out and open the garage door. I swear I'm going to buy an electronic opener—I'll check into it tomorrow."

He hurried out of the car into the thickly falling snow, but his mind was far from electronic garage door openers. Colleen's words were still swirling in his head. She was in love with him, and he had to admit that his behavior these past months had led them to this point. He wanted her to love him, not merely sleep with him. Reeling with insight, he was impervious to the cold wind and icy flakes that swirled around him.

Did he love Colleen? After Donna, he'd decided that love was a word used by the self-deluded to describe relationships based on sex or convenience or perhaps a combination of both. But he hadn't had sex with Colleen and there was nothing particularly convenient about their relationship. He'd had to work harder at winning her trust than he ever had before in his life.

He thought back to Psych 101 and William James's as-if theory. Everybody thought he and Colleen were in love because they'd been acting like a couple in love was supposed to act. Spending time together, laughing, talking, touching, kissing, long, lingering glances and burning gazes. Behavior precedes the emotion. Was he in love, then? It seemed a bizarre prospect for him to contemplate after all his protestations. And yet, and yet . . .

Colleen watched him lift the heavy door then head back toward the car, staggering against the force of the wind. What a disappointing anticlimax her declaration of love had turned out to be! Jack had been stunned into speechlessness, when the most obvious—and natural—response would have been a heartfelt, "I love you too."

But he hadn't said it, because he didn't love her. She'd made a complete fool of herself and now she was stuck here in a blizzard while Jack talked about road conditions and garage door openers, anything to divert the topic from her avowed love for him.

Jack rejoined her in the car long enough to pull it into the garage, then went through the tedious procedure of closing the heavy door again. Colleen ignored him, sitting mute in her seat, until he swung open the door of the Firebird, reached in, and lifted her out.

"What are you doing?" she yelped. "Put me down!"

"I thought you'd find it wildly romantic to be carried inside by the man you profess to love."

She regarded him frostily. "I'm not going to embarrass you or myself any further, Jack, and I'd appreciate it if you wouldn't either." It was difficult to maintain a haughty demeanor while being carried, but she did the best she could, folding her arms and glaring imperiously.

Inside the kitchen, he set her on her feet. She immediately headed for the cherry-red wall phone.

"Who are you calling?" asked Jack.

"Nicola. I hope she'll feel brave enough to venture out and come pick me up."

"You mean suicidal enough. Nobody should be driving in this storm." Jack took the receiver from her hand and replaced it. He began to unbutton her coat. "You're not making any calls tonight, Colleen, and you're not leaving here, either."

Colleen tried unsuccessfully to rebutton it. "The roads aren't too bad yet. I—"

"The roads have nothing to do with it." He slipped the coat from her shoulders and it slid to the floor. "I want you to stay with me tonight, Colleen." He took both her hands in his.

"Because you feel sorry for me because I love you and you don't love me? Well, I don't need a . . . a charity ball, thanks all the same."

"Good, because I have no intention of giving you one." Jack heaved an impatient sigh. "This is not going well at all. I've never bungled anything so badly in my life."

"That's certainly true. I'd think a smooth operator like you would be used to women falling madly in love with you and telling you so. You ought to have some tactful, standard comeback ready—something along the lines of 'I love you, but I'm not in love with you.' One of my brothers-in-law told me he found that one quite effective—before he married my sister, of course."

"Of course." Jack grimaced. "I've used it myself."

"Well, thanks for not using it with me. I'm already mortified enough."

"Believe me, Colleen, the last thing I want you to feel right now is mortified." He drew in a sharp breath. "I guess there is no getting around it. I may as well just say what you want to hear. I—" He paused and cleared his throat. "I love you, Colleen."

Those were the words she'd so badly wanted from him, but not in the way they'd just been offered. She scowled at him. "You're just saying that because you know it's what I want to hear. You even admitted as much."

"I'm saying it because it's the truth. I'm crazy about you, Colleen. I've been in love with you for weeks, but I've been too stupid or too damn stubborn to admit it to myself, let alone to you. But it's true. I love you."

She stared at him, not quite believing what she'd heard. "You—you do?" she breathed.

"Do you think I'd act this idiotic if I weren't in love?" Jack smiled slowly. It was suddenly so obvious, so blindingly clear. "Of course I'm in love with you, Colleen." Still holding her hands, he drew her slowly to him. "It's easy to be cool when you don't care. But I do care, sweetheart, so much. I love you."

"Oh, Jack!" Her voice was husky with joy and wonder and her eyes glistened with tears. She hurled herself at him, wrapping her arms tightly around him, laughing and crying at the same time.

Jack's big hands spanned her waist and he lifted her off her feet and swung her around. Colleen gave a small shriek and they both laughed, their eyes shining with happiness.

"That wasn't so hard." Jack grinned. "Why didn't I just give in and say it weeks ago?"

"I'm glad you didn't. I probably wouldn't have believed you weeks ago. Oh, Jack, I can't remember ever feeling this happy, not even at my sisters' weddings or when my nieces or nephews were born."

Jack's eyes darkened, and he let her body slide slowly down against the long, hard length of him as he lowered her to her feet, turning her release into an extended, intimate caress. "Since I met you I've felt happier than I have in years, Colleen," he said quietly. "You've brightened my life in every way."

She linked her hands around his neck and gazed up at him. "In every way but one," she amended softly. "I want to make love with you, Jack."

They stared at each other for a long moment and then Jack's mouth was on hers, hard and hungry and demanding. It was a demand she answered, her lips parting under his, her tongue seeking his as she kissed him back, her ardor and urgency matching his own.

The more he kissed her, the more she wanted, and when Jack finally lifted his mouth from hers, Colleen clung to him and whispered. "I want you so much, Jack."

Her soft words electrified him. The raging force of his arousal was overwhelming, and primal male instinct urged him to drag her into the nearby living room, push her down onto the thick, cushioned sofa, and bury himself in the softness of her body.

But something stronger than those elemental urges prevailed. He reined in his passion and carried her to his bedroom, setting her gently down in the middle of the big brass bed. A shaft of moonlight lit the room with an otherworldly glow. For the first time in his life, his own pleasure was secondary to his partner's. Colleen needed him to take it slow and easy—and he would, for her. They weren't going to have sex, they were going to make love.

He carefully removed her shoes, one at a time, massaging the insteps of her small feet and tracing the delicate shape of her ankles. "I think I finally understand the appeal of ankle bracelets," he said, his big hand encircling her dainty ankle. "I might even buy you one to wear for me. You have the sexiest ankles in the world."

Quickly kicking off his own shoes, he lay down beside her on the bed. Colleen cuddled close, tracing the sensual line of his mouth with her fingertips. "We're finally together," she said breathlessly. Her lips curved into a loving smile.

Jack gazed down at her. "You're beautiful, Colleen. And so sweet." His fingers worked the buttons of her teal-blue rayon blouse. Her skirt, which was short and tight and matched the blouse perfectly, had slid halfway up her thighs, exposing their shapely firmness.

"And sexy." He groaned, sliding his hand along the length of her leg. His fingers inched under the skirt, pushing it higher. He found and traced the outline of the garter, which was attached to her garter belt. When he caressed the ultrasensitive skin above the tops of her stockings, Colleen shivered in response.

"*Very* sexy." His fingers stroked her. "You have the softest skin," he said huskily. "It feels like silk."

Colleen drew in a shaky breath. She felt flushed; her blood seemed to be burning through her veins like liquid fire. "I—I can hardly believe I'm here," she said, a little shakily. "I've wanted you for such a long time, but I was afraid that you didn't want me."

His laugh was deep and low. "How could you ever think that, baby? I thought I made it very obvious that I wanted you, from the first day we met."

"You made it obvious you wanted to take me to bed. What I was afraid of was that you didn't want me for the right reasons . . . because you love me."

The patterns he was tracing on her inner thighs seemed to be projecting currents of sensual electricity directly to the secret, feminine core of her. She moaned softly, her mind clouding with desire.

"I want you for all the right reasons, sweetheart," he promised. He bent his head, and her mouth opened under his. His tongue penetrated the moist softness, moving deeply in her mouth with an elemental rhythm that she found herself simulating with her hips.

Their kisses grew wilder, more intense. Colleen clung to Jack, her hands moving eagerly over his hard body, wanting to be as close to him as she could be. His hands slipped under her skirt and closed over her derriere. She held her breath as his fingers traced the lacy edges of her panties then audaciously slipped under the silky material to stroke the soft skin beneath.

He pressed her into the taut masculine cradle of his thighs and Colleen felt the heavy pressure of him throb against her as he cupped her rounded softness, as he kneaded and caressed. Deftly, he unfastened the garters, one by one. He rolled down her sheer teal stockings, his hand stroking the length of each leg, pausing to caress the underside of her knee, to learn the shape of her calf, and to fondle her ankles once more.

His dexterity at unhooking her garter belt gave her pause. She couldn't do it as swiftly and easily herself. "You've had a lot of practice at this." Even to her own ears, she'd sounded young and unsure and nervous.

"Don't be afraid of me, Colleen," he said quietly, staring into her wide brown eyes. She looked shyly vulnerable and incredibly sexy, a seemingly impossible combination, yet for her, an effortless one. A wealth of tenderness flooded him. "I love you. Never lose sight of that."

His voice was soft and soothing. He loved her. As she gazed up at him, Colleen could almost feel her insecurities float away, leaving her free and sensual and eager to give everything to the man she loved. Jack Blackledge—the man who loved her, too.

Daringly, she placed her hand against the zipper of his jeans, feeling the hard male bulge beneath the denim. She heard Jack draw a sharp breath and a small smile curved her lips. His immediate response made her feel wonderfully powerful, yet she wanted to please him too. It was a paradox that should have been confusing but somehow wasn't. She felt intensely sexual, wanting to give and to take, to experience, to *know*.

Gently, he removed her hand, pausing to kiss her fingers, her palm, and her wrist before grasping her arm and pulling her to a sitting position. "Take off your blouse for me, Colleen," he commanded softly, his dark eyes sexy and hungry.

The old Colleen would have flinched in embarrassment, but this newly awakened Colleen felt no shame. He had already opened the buttons, so she slipped the blouse from her shoulders.

She was wearing a lacy ecru camisole and her breasts rose, plump and full, over the top of it. Beneath the gossamer silk, her nipples stood out, firm and tightly outlined. Jack reached out and traced the shape of first one and then the other, seemingly fascinated by their size, their shape.

Colleen went weak and soft inside. His mouth brushed hers, lightly at first, and then with increasing demand. And while he was kissing her, long and slow and deep, he cupped her soft breast in his big hand, pulling gently at the nipple, moving his fingers up and down and around until it was tingling with arousal.

Colleen heard herself breathing heavily. Abruptly, she pulled away from Jack, the sensations streaking through her almost too intense to bear. Sensual heat warmed her skin, sensitizing it to such a degree that even the light camisole she was wearing felt constraining and restrictive, an intolerable barrier that had to be removed. She yanked it over her head.

Jack laid her back on the mattress, his eyes smoky and intense. "Your breasts are beautiful, Colleen," he said huskily. "Pink and white, firm and high and so sweetly rounded. I love looking at them. I love touching them."

Colleen watched languidly as the swollen softness of her breasts filled his hands. When his mouth closed hotly, wetly over one rigid, pink-tipped crest, she felt flames of desire lick through her, the churning tension so pleasurable it almost bordered on pain.

He removed her skirt with a one-handed expertise that would have amazed her had she been aware of it. But she wasn't. Her senses were filled with the feel of his warm, wet mouth on her breast and the exquisite sensations pulsing through her as he suckled her. Colleen cried out, clutching him, her nails digging into the heavy knit of his sweater.

His sweater. Suddenly, she found his clothing an unbearable nuisance. She wanted to feel the warmth of his skin against her, she wanted to see him, touch him . . .

She glided her hands up under his sweater, under his shirt, and found the warm bare hardness of his back. She shuddered with need. He felt wonderful, so muscular and strong and male. Her hands wandered around to his chest and tangled in the mat of wiry hair, then inched upward to shyly, tentatively touch his taut nipples.

Jack caught both her hands and pulled them away from him.

Her eyes snapped open and she regarded him anxiously. "Did I do something wrong?"

Jack's response was something between a laugh and a groan. "No, baby. You're doing fine. You're a natural at this. But I'm wearing too many clothes. It's time I shed a few of them."

"How about all of them?" Colleen asked in a sultry, sexy tone she'd never heard herself use before.

He reared back on his knees and pulled off his sweater. Encouraged, Colleen knelt up too and helped him with the buttons of his shirt. Their fingers collided and they missed more buttons than they opened. They broke apart, laughing at their eager ineffectiveness.

"How does that old cliché go? 'Haste makes waste'?" she asked. For just a moment she reflected upon their incredible intimacy. She was kneeling on the bed wearing only her panties, trying to undress him, yet she felt no shame; he was still Jack, whom she could laugh with and tease.

"Unfortunately, clichés happen to be based on truth," Jack said a bit ruefully, tackling the buttons for the second time. This time he completed the job, stripped off his shirt, and tossed it to the floor.

Colleen's eyes moved hungrily over him. His skin glistened with a fine patina of sweat; his chest was broad and solid and covered with a thick mat of jet-black hair that arrowed downward below the waistband of his jeans. She wanted to touch him and she did, running her fingers through the dark tangle, savoring its texture. The scent of his body was faintly musky and it filled her nostrils, intoxicating her.

She watched as he undid the thick buckle of his belt and pulled down the zipper of his jeans. Colleen held her breath, staring in fascination as he disposed of his jeans and underwear with deft precision. Her heart drummed in her chest at the sight of him, naked and standing before her. He was so big, so hard, so powerfully male.

A frisson of fear rippled through her. His blatant masculinity made her feel small and helpless and undeniably vulnerable. She knew the mechanics of lovemaking, of course—but that knowledge suddenly seemed pitifully inadequate.

He sensed her hesitation and once again reined in the wild passion burning inside him. "It's all right, Colleen," he said softly, drawing her back down on the bed with him. "Nothing is going to happen until you want it to happen, until you're ready for it."

Once again, his patience and understanding dissolved her fear. Nude, he lay down beside her and she reached for him. A hot, honeyed warmth flowed from deep within her, spreading through her whole body. Jack's mouth slanted over hers, but this time she took the initiative. Her tongue made a bold foray into his mouth as she kissed him with an intensity previously foreign to her.

His hand trailed amorously across her flat stomach, and she sucked in her breath when his long fingers delved beneath the waistband of her panties. He touched her intimately, finding her damp and swollen. Colleen trembled violently.

He slipped off her panties and she was naked and clinging to him. He smoothed his palm over her stomach, and she closed her eyes tightly, waiting for him to move it lower, wanting it with a yearning desperation. She was quivering, and a hot, syrupy warmth flowed through her, making her moist and pliant.

"Jack." She cried his name as an enormous wave of passionate need crashed through her. "Jack, please."

"Do you want me to touch you?" he asked thickly. She was too inexperienced to mask her need and her unbridled display of arousal delighted him. She was marvelously, innately sensual, so passionate. He could take her now, but he wanted to spin out the loveplay until she was so hot and hungry for him that any lingering apprehension would be swept away in a malestrom of passion.

"Where do you want me to touch you, Colleen?" he murmured. "Here?" His rough palm covered the silken triangle of dark gold curls at the apex of her thighs.

She made a small sound and her eyes flew open. He was watching her, his eyes fierce with desire. "Yes," she managed, stirring languorously under his hand.

"Open your legs for me, Colleen," he ordered sexily, and she went hot all over. But the empty ache inside her and her own pulsing excitement immediately banished any inhibitions.

Daringly, she relaxed her legs, moving them slightly apart and his finger probed between the soft folds, lightly stroking. His mouth captured hers while he continued his sensual exploration, and Colleen's head spun. The way he was touching her . . . the way he was making her feel . . . She never wanted it to stop, and yet something was building inside her, something unfamiliar, elusive, but wildly exciting.

She tore her mouth from his. "Jack, I—"

Whatever she'd been about to say was abruptly forgotten as he slowly slid his finger inside her. Colleen shuddered convulsively. She clenched around him weakly but instinctively and the sensation was so exquisitely pleasurable that she did it again.

"You're so soft and wet and tight," Jack said, his voice deep and low. His entire body was throbbing. "I never dreamed I could want anyone or anything as much as I want you, Colleen."

"It's the same for me"—she gasped—"with you." There was a tension and a fever rising in her, making her shiver and cling to him. Her body arched into his, her hips undulating in a sexy, natural rhythm. Between her legs was an emptiness that demanded to be filled. "Love me, Jack," she pleaded softly. "Love me now."

"I might hurt you." His voice was raspy in the dark stillness.

Colleen felt the tension pounding through him, sensed the iron control keeping him in check. "I don't care," she whispered, her lips brushing his. "I love you so much, I want you so much, it'll be worth it."

"I have to protect you," he said, and she heard a rustling of foil. She was grateful he had the presence of mind to think of it, for she hadn't given it a thought. Her own inexperience next to his sexual sophistication momentarily unnerved her once again.

Jack moved between her legs and Colleen held her breath as she felt him against her, hard and burning. Their eyes met and held in the muted moonlight that streamed across the bed.

He sank into her, pushing past the fragile barrier, murmuring love words and sex words, tender and exciting in turn as they swirled around in her head. Colleen lay still, accepting his slow, deep penetration, tensing once during a spasm of pain.

"Relax, sweetheart," Jack crooned softly. His voice was mesmerizingly seductive; his warm breath fanned her face. He kissed her cheeks and tasted the salt of her tears. "It's all right, my sweet baby. Just relax for me."

Colleen breathed deeply, feeling enormous pressure as her body stretched itself to adjust to him. A small, scared part of her wanted to fight him, to push him away, but she didn't give in to the fear, choosing instead to listen to Jack's soft words, to focus on how much she loved him. And slowly, gradually, she relaxed. Her body began to accustom itself to him as he rested still and deep inside her.

When he started to move within her, she tensed a little, expecting pain, but there was none, just the gliding pressure of heat and longing, of raw, primitive excitement that built and built as she clung to him. Her arms and legs were wrapped tightly around him as he filled and refilled her soft depths, making her moan and cry out with the sheer, savage pleasure of it.

As they moved together, the sensuous rhythm of their movements grew harder and faster. Colleen felt a hot spiral of tension deep within her begin to wind tighter and tighter until it sprang loose, sending wild waves of shuddering, clenching pleasure crashing through her. She felt his body convulse as his virile strength surged into her, she heard the sound of her name on his lips as it happened, and she knew a joy and fulfillment she had never before experienced.

They were silent for a long while afterward, feeling so close that no words were needed between them. Colleen lay cradled in Jack's arms, a glowing warm languor radiating throughout her entire body. She breathed a drowsy sigh and snuggled into his hard, warm strength.

"I guess there is something to all that love-and-sex business after all," said Jack, his voice warm with affection. He stroked her long blond hair with gentle hands. "This can't compare to anything else."

She smiled up at him, her face alive with warmth and tenderness. "That's the second most wonderful thing you could say to me, Jack."

"What's the first?"

"You already said it." She sighed happily. "I love you."

"Then I'll say it again. I love you, Colleen."

They kissed lazily, lingeringly. And soon after, fell asleep in each other's arms.

Ten

The shrill ringing of the telephone awakened them the next morning. Jack opened one eye, glanced at his bedside clock and groaned. 7:31. Who on earth would be calling him at the ungodly hour of 7:31 on a Saturday morning?

"Yeah?" he barked into the phone.

Colleen, who had been draped over him, sleepily sat up in bed. Her big brown eyes traveled over her unfamiliar surroundings. This was the first time in her life she'd ever awakened in a man's bed, in a man's arms. She'd spent the night here, cuddling close to Jack under the thick goose-down quilt. Here in the early morning light, the hot passion of last night seemed as far away as the midnight darkness. Last night . . .

Just thinking about it made her go hot and weak inside. She clutched the sheet around her, excruciatingly aware of her nakedness. She felt so very vulnerable, so very shy.

When Jack heaved a sudden impatient groan, Colleen flinched and her fingers tightened around the protective drape of the sheet.

"It's for you. It's Nicola," he announced crankily. He handed her the phone, then rolled onto his stomach and pulled the pillow over his head.

Colleen's heart thumped. "Nicola? Anything wrong?"

"Three and a half feet of snow outside and you ask if there's anything wrong." Nicola said dryly. "The whole city is snowed in, Colleen. There are drifts up to seven feet out there. Take a look outside the window if you haven't yet."

"I haven't yet," Colleen mumbled. "Uh, did you call to issue a weather bulletin, Nic?"

"Worse. I called to issue a Brady/Ramsey bulletin. You know what early risers they are, Colleen. Apparently, they caught the weather on TV this morning, and even though they're way down there in Texas, Buffalo's forty-inch snowfall grabbed their attention. Shavonne, Erin, and Tara have all called to ask if you're faring okay up here in the frozen north—and to offer plane tickets back to Houston as soon as the airport reopens."

Colleen sat stock-still. "What did you tell them, Nicola? Where did you say I was?" There weren't too many options at such an early hour on a Saturday morning with the city paralyzed by a humongous snowstorm.

"I said you'd spent the night with a girlfriend from work, that you were snowed in at her house but had called to tell me you were fine."

Colleen breathed a sigh of relief. "Thanks a million, Nic. I—"

"It's not that easy, Colleen. It never is when it comes to our families, remember? Your sisters wanted the name of the friend and her phone number so they could call you there, just to reassure themselves that you really are okay."

Colleen gulped. "Oh, Nicola!"

"I pretended that I couldn't remember the name of the friend, so I couldn't give them a number. But they didn't buy it, Colleen. Your sister Megan just called. She said your older sisters are frantic and the brothers-in-law are about to step in. They're certain you're in some kind of dire trouble. Apparently they're convinced that I would *never* not know exactly where you are and who you're with—that's what you get for being responsible, reliable, and scrupulously honest all your life. Megan is a little more realistic. She said she knows you're with a guy, and would you please call Houston immediately and calm them all down."

Colleen looked at Jack's long length under the covers. There wasn't an inch of him that was visible, but she knew he could hear every word. She swallowed. She was not at all well versed in what to do and say the morning after a passionate night before. "Call them immediately?" She lowered her voice. "This could be embarrassing, Nicola."

"I sympathize completely," Nicola said consolingly. "Kamal answered the phone this morning when my brother Alex called at six. What a precarious moment that was! I told Alex he was the landlord, making sure our pipes hadn't frozen during the night."

"Kamal is at our apartment? He spent the night with you?"

"He came over after he called last night. He was worried about me being alone during the big snow."

Colleen coughed. "I see. Well, thanks for calling, Nic. I'll talk to you later."

Did Nicola know what she was doing? At that particular moment, Colleen wasn't sure if she herself knew what she was doing, either. For Nicola's warning call had brought into sharp focus several things that had not been resolved between her and Jack last night . . . his plans to marry a rich wife, if he married at all. And the existence of her own money and her relationship to the super-rich Ramseys.

She leaned over Jack to replace the receiver in its cradle. "Jack, do you mind if I—uh—make a few long-distance calls?"

He sat up in bed, grabbed her wrists, and pulled her down on top of him. "You bet I mind." He rolled over on top of her, his mouth hovering above hers.

His dark eyes gleamed. "This is no time to be talking on the phone, woman. You have a hot, horny man in your bed who demands your complete attention."

"Oh dear." Colleen bit her lip. She'd never had to put anyone before her family before, and now Jack wanted her to do just that. "I—I really ought to call my sisters." He was nibbling on her neck and the hard, warm weight of him upon her was affecting her like an aphrodisiac. "But—but maybe I could wait a little while . . ."

"A long while," Jack amended. His mouth took hers in a consuming kiss, and Colleen responded to him with all the newly awakened passion within her.

The fires flared and burned between them with passionate intensity, thrusting them both out of this world and into another sensual, rapturous dimension. Colleen moved with him and for him, and the swirling pleasure and heat carried her higher and higher, out of herself, to the high planes of soul-shattering ecstasy. Jack was with her all the way.

It was another couple hours before she actually got around to making the phone calls. First came a nap in which she lay in Jack's arms replete with contentment, then a sensuous soak in the whirlpool with him. He was making breakfast—microwaved pancakes and coffee—when she hurriedly placed a call to her oldest sister, Shavonne.

"I'm fine, Shavonne. It was sweet of you and the others to worry about me, though," Colleen said with what she hoped was credible sincerity, all the while casting a watchful eye toward the bedroom door.

Jack was in the kitchen, but she didn't want him to come in and hear her telling her sister that she'd spent the night with Susan Farley. She felt guilty about lying to her sister, guilty about her lie of omission to Jack. Lying in his arms, she'd felt every inch a mature woman; now, on the phone, she felt like a naughty little girl.

"Colleen, won't you please reconsider and come back home?" Shavonne pleaded. "We miss you so much, we all do. And with all that horrible weather up there—"

"I like it here, Shavonne, I really do," insisted Colleen. "And I miss all of you too, but—"

"You have a boyfriend up there, don't you, Colleen?" Shavonne said perceptively. "Why haven't you ever mentioned him to us?"

Colleen sighed. *Why hadn't she?* Her reasons were all tied in with the Ramsey money and her uncertainty about how Jack would react. And she knew if she were to tell her family that she was seriously involved with someone, they would all be up on the next plane to check him out, just like Jack's mother and aunts. Except there was an enormous difference between those three dear ladies and her powerful Ramsey in-laws.

"I am—uh—seeing someone regularly," Colleen admitted.

"I knew it!" Shavonne exclaimed, her voice lively with interest. "Tell me all about him, Colleen."

Colleen couldn't resist the thrill of talking about her new love, and she found herself telling Shavonne about Jack Blackledge.

Shavonne listened carefully, not making many comments or asking many questions, just letting Colleen talk on about him. "You're really hung up on this guy, aren't you, Colleen?" she said at last. She sounded worried.

"Not hung up on," Colleen contradicted her. *Hung up on* described Nicola's torturous feelings for the out-of-reach Kamal. "I'm in love with him, Shavonne."

She heard her sister suck in her breath. "Colleen, you're very young, and you haven't known him all that long. Why, you've only been in Buffalo—"

"I've been here long enough to know I love Jack,

Shavonne," Colleen said fiercely. "Megan was much younger than I am now when she married Ricky, and I remember how all of you tried to keep them apart, so if you or the Ramseys are entertaining any similar plots of breaking us up—"

"Colleen, you're being overdramatic. You just told me about this person. How could we be *entertaining a plot* to break you up?"

"Just don't try it," Colleen said firmly.

Jack appeared in the doorway. "Breakfast," he called. "Come eat the pancakes before they turn completely to stone. They're already slightly petrified around the edges. I think I microwaved them a tad too long."

"Colleen, is that a man's voice?" demanded Shavonne.

"It's—he's—um—the landlord," Colleen said quickly, giving mental thanks to Nicola for coming up with that one. "He's come to check that the pipes aren't frozen. It's—a very common custom here in Buffalo."

Jack laughed. Colleen blushed and quickly got off the phone. "I don't possess the necessary aplomb to casually tell my big sister that I'm in a man's bedroom—the same one I spent the night in," she admitted sheepishly.

"I understand completely. I have a family too, remember?" He opened his arms to her, and she rushed into them, burying her face in his chest and hugging him tight.

"I love you so much, Jack."

"Sweetheart." He smiled down at her, then kissed her soundly.

When they finally reached the kitchen a long while later, they disposed of the solidified pancakes and put two grilled-cheese-sandwich-and-tomato-soup meals in the microwave. Jack pronounced them cooked to perfection, and Colleen proclaimed that it was by far the most delicious meal she'd ever eaten.

They spent the rest of the weekend together, snow-bound, and enjoyed every moment of their captivity.

November continued as a sweet, love-filled dream for Colleen. She spent almost every waking moment with Jack—and every sleeping moment, too. He made room in his closet for some of her clothes; her toothbrush and cosmetics shared space on the bathroom counter with his personal items. Her favorite cookies and frozen chicken pot pies were in his kitchen, her magazines were mixed with his in his den.

Whole days passed without her needing to return to her apartment, and when she did, it was usually to pick up more of her things and take them over to Jack's. His place felt more like home these days, Colleen mused, especially since Kamal Veli's clothes, toothbrush, and toiletries, his favorite foods and books had come to occupy space in her apartment. Her former apartment, Colleen corrected herself, which Nicola was now sharing unofficially with Kamal, just as Colleen was unofficially sharing Jack's house.

Sometimes Colleen was content with the arrangement and sometimes she wished they would progress from the unofficial to the official. Her wish intensified as the Thanksgiving holidays approached. She and Jack and Nicola and Kamal made plans to have a traditional Thanksgiving dinner at Jack's house, with everything cooked from scratch, not one microwavable item on the menu. Colleen had a notebook of recipes and cooking advice from Stefanie Doebler, the indomitable food editor.

Unfortunately, there was a mighty roar and cry from her family when she announced her intentions to stay in Buffalo for the holiday and not return to Houston for the traditional Thanksgiving feast held in patriarch Quentin Ramsey's River Oaks mansion.

Nicola fell under a similar wall of protests from the Shakarians.

Colleen and Nicola stood firm and held to their original plans, but there was definitely a damper on their anticipation of the holiday. "The last thing I want to do is disappoint my family," Colleen said sadly to Nicola as they met to go over their Thanksgiving shopping list.

"No, that's the *next* to the last thing," Nicola pointed out practically. "The *last* thing you want to do is go to Houston and leave Jack here in Buffalo alone over Thanksgiving."

She would not be swayed, Colleen vowed after the latest phone call from Houston. Not by the announcement of her sister Tara's first pregnancy. Not by the news that her nieces Carrie Beth and Courtney had landed starring roles in their school play. Not by Megan and her husband Rick's intended plans to apply jointly to law school. Not even by Shavonne and Erin's impassioned declarations that Thanksgiving wouldn't be the same without her.

After all, Colleen reasoned, she would be going to Houston for a week at Christmastime. She would be there for Carrie Beth's and Courtney's play; Tara's baby wasn't due for eight months, and Megan and Ricky had announced plans last year to apply jointly to medical school. As of yet, they were still both working in the marketing department of Ramsey & Sons.

The Brady/Ramsey clan could survive a Thanksgiving without her very nicely, Colleen explained patiently and politely to both Erin and Shavonne. But she and Jack wanted to be together; they needed to be.

"This is the best Thanksgiving I've ever had." Colleen sighed happily as she and Jack stood at the doorway, bidding good-bye to Nicola and Kamal.

"The dinner was perfect, and we only had to make two emergency calls to Stefanie Doebler for help."

"It was a delicious meal," Jack agreed, leaning down to kiss her lips lightly.

Colleen sighed. This was what it must be like to be married, she thought wistfully—entertaining friends at home, then discussing the evening afterward, going to bed together. They walked to the bedroom hand in hand, talking desultorily, a passionate excitement building as they exchanged glances, kisses, love words.

She wished they were married or maybe engaged or at least talking about getting engaged. But they lived day to day and marriage was never mentioned. Sometimes Colleen pondered over how to bring up the subject without sounding pushy or desperate or both; plus, the problem of introducing her true financial worth seemed insurmountable. What could she say? *"Do you still want to marry a rich woman, Jack? Well, guess what? I am one."*

No, she wasn't about to rock the boat. There was no need. She loved Jack and he loved her and that was the most important thing. She had to believe that in time everything would work out for the best. She *knew* that it would, she loved him so. And he loved her.

Colleen gazed up at him, her heart in her eyes, and Jack picked her up and laid her on the bed. "You're irresistible," he said softly, wonderingly. No matter how much time they spent together, she never ceased to captivate him, to charm him. And no matter how often they made love, it only grew more wonderful, more intense and profoundly satisfying.

"Go back to sleep, sweetheart. You can work here today. I'm only going in for a couple of hours." Jack leaned down and kissed her as she lay drowsing in the big brass bed.

There was only a skeleton crew of reporters on hand the Friday after Thanksgiving, most staffers having finished their feature articles ahead of time so they could take an additional day off.

Jack was at his desk, on his second cup of coffee and first rewrite, when the tall, gray-haired man in an expensive Burberry trench coat approached him. "Jackson Blackledge?"

Jack looked up at him. "That's me."

"I'm Quentin Ramsey." The man's smoke-gray eyes were as cold and as hard as steel. He didn't offer his hand to shake, he just stood staring down at Jack with his icy gray eyes.

Defensively, uneasily, Jack rose to his feet. "What can I do for you?" He almost called the man sir, for Ramsey had a natural commanding air that demanded deference. But Jack realized that this man intended to intimidate him and he was not about to cede him any concessions, however small.

"Don't pretend that you don't know who I am," snapped Quentin Ramsey. "Kindly spare us both that nauseating act. I'll cut straight to the chase." He reached inside his coat pocket and pulled out a check, which he thrust in front of Jack.

It was a cashier's check for one million dollars. Jack smiled sardonically. "Are we on camera or something? Is somebody making a video of people gaping, gasping, and doing pratfalls over bogus million-dollar checks?"

"It's not bogus. It's real and it's yours," Ramsey said coolly, placing the check on Jack's desk. "You can go to any bank and cash it immediately."

"Yeah, right. And all I have to do is . . ." Jack paused, waiting, wondering who and what this was all about. Still thinking it was a practical joke, one he was determined not to fall for, he kept his cool and smiled insolently. "I'm sure there are certain strings attached to this check."

"There are," Quentin Ramsey said bluntly. "Keep away from Colleen Brady."

Jack gaped at him. Suddenly the joke didn't seem all that funny anymore. "Hey," he began. "What's this—"

"We Ramseys know all about you, Blackledge, and I know you know who we are, so let's skip the games," Ramsey interrupted coldly. "When Colleen refused to come home for Thanksgiving, her sisters, my daughters-in-law, were plenty upset, and I don't like to see the mothers of my grandchildren upset. I'm also personally fond of Colleen; she's family. She's a sweet, decent little girl, and I won't have her used or corrupted. I put a private investigator on your tail, and none of us liked the report we got back. You know what was in it—information verifying that you're a self-stated fortune hunter who's said countless times to anybody who would listen that you intend to marry a rich wife."

Jack opened his mouth to protest, then abruptly closed it. He had said that. But had he ever once considered the ramifications of such a statement? The answer was a resounding no. He knew at this moment that he'd merely been spouting off, showing off, building up his ego, which had been dented by Donna's defection. He had no ego problems now; he was in love with a wonderful girl for the first time in his life and—

"I will not hesitate to do everything within my power,"—Quentin Ramsey's quiet, menacing voice cut into his reverie—"and I do have considerable power, Blackledge, to make sure that Colleen Brady isn't victimized by fortune-hunting slime such as yourself."

"Hi!" Colleen called gaily as she heard Jack come into the house. She rushed to meet him, ready to jump into his arms. And then she saw his expression. "Jack, what's wrong?" she asked with a gasp. She'd never seen him look so—so *forbidding*, not even in the earliest, stormiest days of their relationship.

"Nothing's wrong, Colleen." He held out a check. "I'm a rich man. I don't even have to go through with my nefarious scheme of marrying a defenseless, naive millionairess. Quentin Ramsey himself came to the office today to buy you out of our relationship."

"Quentin Ramsey?" Colleen squeaked. "He's in Buffalo?" Her stomach jumped as her heart plummeted. They seemed to meet in a sickening collision somewhere in her midsection.

"He was. He jetted in and out in the family corporate jet." Jack surveyed her stricken countenance with a cool, mocking smile. "When—if ever—did you intend to tell me that you were related to one of the richest families in the country, Colleen? At the same time that you divulged your own personal net worth?"

"Jack, I wanted to tell you, but—but there never seemed to be a right time to bring it up and—"

"Colleen, we've been together twenty-four hours a day for weeks, for months! We've talked about everything. Everything, it seems, except this lie you've been living."

"I haven't been living a lie!" Colleen cried.

"What would you call playing at a low-paying job, sharing an apartment with a hard-working, penny-saving nurse—or is Nicola a secret heiress too? Suckering a guy who fell for your little act hook, line, and sinker? While all the while you're a little rich girl who could buy and sell me several times over, who was playing around—maybe slumming is more apt—until you got bored and returned to your rich family and your rich-girl life and the rich guy the Ramseys have all picked out for you."

"You can't believe any of that, Jack," Colleen said tremulously. "I don't know what Quentin told you, but—"

"He gave me this check and told me to stay away

from you. His private investigator has solid evidence that I am a fortune hunter. The PI has names and quotes from a number of people who heard me say I intended to marry for money."

"We both know you weren't even aware that I—I'm sort of a Ramsey and have some Ramsey money," Colleen interjected hotly. "Why didn't you just rip up the check and tell Quentin to mind his own business?"

"He warned me against making any such 'grand gestures,' as he called it, in hopes of getting more money by marrying you. The Ramseys have influential friends in high places, it seems. Big Daddy Quentin can personally make a few phone calls and ensure that I never work in the newspaper business again, anywhere in the country. He'll do it if I don't get out of your life immediately."

Colleen sank into a nearby chair. She was too shocked and felt too sick even to cry. "So you decided to take the easy way out? To take the check, keep your job, and dump me?"

"What do I want with a spoiled little rich girl who doesn't trust me enough to tell me the truth about herself?"

Colleen closed her eyes. It was too awful to contemplate, it just couldn't be true! "You—you don't want me anymore? You'd rather have Quentin's check instead of me?"

Jack turned and walked out of the room.

It was by coincidence that Nicola stopped at the house just a few minutes later to pick up the pie pan and salad bowl she'd left there after Thanksgiving dinner. Colleen burst into tears at the sight of her, grabbed her coat, and insisted upon leaving with her.

She spent the night in her bedroom in her apartment, trying to ignore the fact that Nicola and Kamal were in the next room trying, not very successfully, to make love silently. They had both been so nice to her, comforting her, trying to cheer her up. Kamal had even said he was glad she was moving back because he knew how much Nicola had missed her company. A lie, but a well-meaning one, and Colleen had cried harder.

She did her best to rejoice in the news that Kamal had ended his engagement to the girl in Azerbaijan and that Nicola had told her family about Kamal and they hadn't gone berserk, after all. Since he wasn't Turkish and hadn't been personally involved in the Azerbaijani-Armenian war, the Shakarians had decided they could accept him.

She was glad that Nicola's life had taken a turn for the better, even though her own had taken a turn for the worse, Colleen thought bleakly. She'd never subscribed to the misery-loves-company school of thought.

Every time the phone rang, Colleen told Nicola that she didn't want to talk to Jack, that she wouldn't take any calls from him, but the point was moot because he didn't call that night or the next day or the next. Her family did, though, and Colleen refused to talk to any of them, either.

"Your interference has ruined Colleen's life," she heard Nicola sternly tell Shavonne, then Erin, then Tara, then Megan, and finally Quentin Ramsey himself. "Is it any wonder that she doesn't want to see, hear, or speak to a single Ramsey?"

Colleen sent Nicola and Kamal to Jack's house to retrieve her things early Sunday afternoon, giving them her key to the place and praying that he wouldn't let them take anything, that he would immediately come over to bring her home, to tell her that he loved her, that all was forgiven, that Quentin Ramsey's poisonous check was in the mail—in a thousand pieces—winging its way back to Houston.

But Nicola and Kamal returned with her things. Jack hadn't even been at home. Colleen put her belongings away in a state of total despair.

When the telephone rang and Nicola informed her it was Rodd Garrett, she almost declined the call.

But Nicola urged her to talk to him, and as usual, he was nice—funny, pleasant, and easy to talk to. He asked her to go to Harry's Sports Bar with him and some of his friends later that evening.

Colleen almost reflexively refused, but not before some cruel facts leaped to mind: She'd been dumped, and Jack wasn't at home. Was he with another woman, a continuation of last night's date? her heart cried. Kamal and Nicola had theater tickets for tonight and would be gone for the evening.

Did she really want to spend this evening alone, trying to watch television while contemplating the emptiness of her life?

Colleen accepted Rodd Garrett's invitation.

Eleven

Colleen was sorry from the moment Rodd picked her up that she'd agreed to go. He seemed preoccupied, sullen almost, and disinclined to talk. He slipped a cassette into the car's tape player and turned up the volume so loud that conversation was impossible anyway. The music filled what otherwise would have been an awkward silence.

Harry's Sports Bar was packed with a lively, noisy crowd, almost all of whom seemed to know Rodd. Many were teammates, their dates, or wives and there was a numerous contingent of Bills' fans as well. Colleen fought back a choking wave of grief as memories of the times she'd spent here with Jack flooded her. The first time they'd made love was the same evening when they had argued at Harry's— over Rodd Garrett. There seemed to be a kind of symmetry to it, leading to this miserable, heart-breaking moment.

A continuous parade of people joined Rodd and Colleen at their table to joke and laugh and help themselves to the Buffalo chicken wings that Rodd kept ordering. They never did get around to ordering dinner, just endless rounds of the Buffalo specialty and plate after plate of ranch fries.

And beer. So much beer.

Colleen gave up counting the number of pitchers brought to their table and the number of times Rodd filled, drained, and then refilled his glass. She tried to be a good sport, chatting with Rodd's friends and laughing at their jokes, which seemed to grow more and more inane as the evening progressed. She didn't like beer and stuck to Diet Coke, which did not please Rodd at all. He tried to ridicule her into drinking, and when she firmly resisted, he ignored her and turned his full attention to his friends.

After three interminable hours, Colleen knew it was definitely time to leave. The beer was having a strange effect on Rodd; not only did it make him drunk, it completely changed his personality. Under its influence he became mean and belligerent and overbearing, so very different from the amiable, good-natured man he usually was. She decided to call Nicola to ask her to pick her up, hoping against hope that she and Kamal would be back from the theater. But when she stood to leave the table, Rodd bellowed, "Where the hell do you think you're going?"

"To make a phone call," Colleen replied. Her stomach was churning, and she realized that she was afraid of Rodd Garrett. The sooner she left, the better.

Rodd reached across the table and forcibly pushed her back into her seat. "Sit down, Belinda. You ain't goin' nowhere." He laughed harshly and gulped down the rest of the beer in his mug, then shouted to the harried waitress for another round.

"Hey, Rodd, she's not Belinda," one of the men at their table told him. "She's—uh—what's your name, honey?"

"Colleen," she mumbled. Her heart was pounding, and she felt a chill of real fear. Rodd Garrett was built like a tank, and the thought of all that strength used against her was terrifying. "Who's Belinda?"

"She's a bitch!" shouted Rodd, and let loose with a string of scorching curses.

"Belinda went with Rodd for a couple years," Tina, the fiancée of a mammoth defensive lineman murmured to Colleen. "It looked serious for a while, but she broke it off a few months ago." Tina lowered her voice to a barely audible whisper. "Belinda said she couldn't take his partying all the time. She's going with someone else now and Rodd took it hard, though he won't admit it. You sort of look like her."

For partying read drinking, thought Colleen, and sympathized with the unseen Belinda. But it was unsettling to learn of her resemblance to the other woman. It made Rodd Garrett's behavior even scarier. Colleen pushed her chair away from the table and got up quickly, out of Rodd's range. "I have to leave."

"Okay, okay!" Rodd stood up too. "I'll take you."

Colleen's eyes widened in alarm. "He can't drive in that condition." She appealed to Tina, one of the few in the crowd who wasn't drunk or halfway there.

Tina nodded her agreement. "You'd better get his car keys and drive him home."

Colleen grimaced. Driving Rodd Garrett wasn't quite what she had in mind. "He'll never give me the keys," she said anxiously.

"Trane, get Rodd's keys and give them to Colleen," Tina ordered. "She's driving him home tonight."

Trane was even bigger than Rodd, and apparently, Rodd wasn't so drunk that he didn't realize the folly of defying the building-size hulk's command to hand over the keys. He did, and Trane gave them to Colleen.

Colleen chewed her lower lip. "I don't know where he lives." She glanced over at Rodd, who had just smashed a beer can into his forehead, crushing it and then hooting with triumph.

She remembered how affable and courteous he had been that evening at Niagara Falls with Jack's mother and aunt and the children at his nephew's birthday party, how nice he'd been during their talks on the telephone. She'd never dreamed he could turn into this loud, barbarous stranger. "He doesn't seem to be in any shape to give me directions, either," she added glumly.

Tina sighed. "I know where he lives. I'll drive Trane's car, and you can follow me to Rodd's place. Trane, give me your keys, sugar, I need your car. You stay here and wait for me."

Trane docilely handed over the keys. "Come on, Rodd, Colleen's gonna drive you home," Tina ordered in a voice that brooked no argument.

To Colleen's relief, Rodd followed them outside without protest and climbed into the passenger side of his Ferrari. She thanked Tina profusely and tried not to think what she would have done if the other woman hadn't come to her aid.

Colleen was grateful that she'd had the opportunity to drive the various Ramsey sports cars or she would have had an anxiety attack driving the powerful Ferrari. She drove slower than the speed limit, which caused Rodd to berate her driving prowess until he dozed off, slumping heavily in his seat.

Tina finally slowed to a halt in front of a two-story brick Colonial-style house in a quiet, tree-lined residential neighborhood. "That's it," she called, leaning out the car window and pointing.

Before Colleen could roll down her window and ask for a ride home, Tina gunned the car's engine and was gone.

Colleen glanced over at Rodd, who was snoring loudly. Now what? she wondered, irritation replacing the anxiety that had been building steadily. What a perfectly awful night this had been, a fitting complement to what had turned into the worst weekend of her life. The future didn't hold much promise either; it loomed bleak and lonely without Jack. It seemed her life was on a downward spiral, courtesy of Quentin Ramsey and his overly aggressive, meddling clan. A combination of gloom and anger weighed heavily upon her.

Sighing, Colleen pulled into the driveway of

Rodd's house, right up to the door of the attached garage, but she saw no automatic garage door opener in the car. Apparently Rodd, like Jack, hadn't invested in one.

The irrelevant thought brought tears to her eyes and Colleen gulped back a sob. Rodd could stay in the car and sleep it off, she decided, fighting the tears. She was tired of crying. Her eyes burned and her throat was sore from the prolonged bouts of weeping. She had cried too much since Jack had kicked her out of his life. Jaw quivering, Colleen headed inside the house to call Nicola for a ride.

The second key she tried fit the lock on the front door, and Colleen entered the house. It was totally dark inside, and she groped in the blackness until her eyes had adjusted, then quickly switched on the first light she could find.

It was strange, being alone in Rodd's house, a place she'd never been before. She felt as stealthy as a cat burglar, going from room to room looking for a phone. She finally located one in a huge black, red, and white bedroom on the second floor. There was a gigantic water bed on a platform in the middle of the room and a mirror and a trapeze affixed to the ceiling above the bed.

Colleen gaped at the trapeze. She didn't even want to imagine what that was used for! She couldn't get out of here fast enough. She grabbed the phone and quickly called her apartment, willing Nicola to answer. Hopefully, she and Kamal had returned directly to her apartment after the play . . .

She let it ring and ring ten, eleven, twelve times, finally concluding that either Nicola and Kamal weren't there or else they weren't answering. Once again, apprehension began to build within Colleen. She dialed directory assistance and got the numbers of two taxi companies. Both told her that it would be at least a ninety-minute wait before a cab could be dispatched.

After she hung up, Colleen realized that she didn't

even know the address. She hadn't been paying attention to street signs and numbers on the drive over here; she'd been concentrating on keeping the Ferrari under control.

Colleen sank down onto the water bed, then gripped the sides as it pitched and rolled beneath her. As far as she could see, she had only one option left. Calling Jack. She needed a ride home, and he would know where Rodd lived. She really had no choice, Colleen assured herself; this was not merely an excuse to see him. She had some pride, after all, enough to keep her from throwing herself at a man who didn't want her. No, this was a practical matter, divorced from the personal. Her fingers shaking, Colleen dialed Jack's number.

He picked up on the third ring. "Yeah?"

She'd never been so glad to hear his voice in her life. All the love she felt for him flared like a torch, lighting a spark of hope inside her.

"Jack, this is Colleen," she said breathlessly.

"There's no need to identify yourself," he drawled. "I haven't forgotten the sound of your voice quite yet."

Did he expect a cool, glib response? If so, Colleen knew she couldn't deliver. "Jack, I—I'm in trouble and I have a big favor to ask," she said bluntly. "I'm stuck . . . somewhere, and I need a ride."

He responded at once to the urgency in her voice. "Where are you, Colleen?"

She drew a deep breath. "At Rodd Garrett's house. And I don't know the address."

There was a long, charged silence. And then Jack's voice, cold and caustic: "Let Rodd take you home. I don't provide taxi service for his dates."

"Jack, please don't hang up!" Her voice broke. "I'm scared. He's passed out in the car and—"

"Belinda!" The name seemed to reverberate through the house. A door slammed and there came a sound of something falling, as if it had been knocked over, followed by a string of foul curses.

Colleen froze. "It's him! He's inside."

"Where are you, bitch?" Rodd Garrett shouted so loudly that Jack heard him over the line.

"Colleen, what's going on?" Jack demanded.

"He's drunk out of his mind," Colleen whispered frantically. "I'm afraid of him, Jack. Please come now."

Jack muttered a curse, then said, "I'll leave right away. Colleen, keep away from him. Lock yourself in somewhere."

Colleen barely had time to replace the receiver and run to the adjacent bathroom before Rodd appeared in the doorway of the bedroom. "Come 'ere!" he demanded, his voice thick.

She slammed the bathroom door and locked it, her heart beating so fast and so hard that she felt faint.

Rodd began to pound on the door. "Open up, Belinda. You'll be damn sorry if you don't!"

"I'm not Belinda, I'm Colleen," she tried desperately. "Remember our date tonight?"

"Get out here, bitch! Right now!" The pounding grew louder and more forceful, and the door shook ominously.

He was throwing himself against the door like a battering ram, Colleen realized in horror. Could a wooden door, and not a particularly thick one at that, withstand the force of Rodd Garrett's tremendous strength?

"I'm kicking in the door!" he warned furiously. There was an ear-splitting crash and the door bulged forward, but it still managed to hold.

Not for long, though, Colleen was certain of that. She jumped into the bathtub, an elaborate, oversize tile-and-marble whirlpool, which was out of range of Rodd and the door. She had never been so frightened in her entire life; she was shaking and could hardly breathe. Every time she inhaled, it felt as if knives were cutting into her chest.

A minute later the door came flying through the

air, with Rodd Garrett right behind it. The force of his kick propelled him into the far wall, giving her a few precious seconds to bolt from the bathroom.

She was halfway through the bathroom, on her way to the door, when he caught her with a belly-smacking tackle. Colleen hit the floor, hard, Rodd coming down with her.

"So you like it rough, huh, baby?" He laughed and began to press wet, beery kisses on her neck.

The impact of her fall had winded her and for a few seconds Colleen lay still, gasping for air. The whole room seemed to be spinning in a sickening whirl, but a fresh burst of adrenaline enabled her to kick him and pound at him with her fists. She twisted her neck back and forth to avoid his seeking mouth.

Rodd laughed, seeming to take pleasure in her struggles, fending off her blows and pinning her down with his tree-trunk thighs and steely arms. The smell of sweat and beer suffused her nostrils, further nauseating her. She was wild with fear and pain, and as his horrible mouth descended over hers, she bit down on his tongue with all her might.

Rodd emitted a furious, indignant howl, rolled off her, and sat up. "You bit me!" he roared. His eyes looked like tiny slits in his big face, which was contorted with rage. He touched his hand to his mouth and recoiled at the sight of blood. "I'm bleeding!" he bawled, and drawing back his hand, he hit her across the cheek.

A white flash of pain momentarily blinded her, but Colleen took advantage of her freedom to scramble to her feet. Rodd lumbered after her; but he was too drunk to be fast or well coordinated, while she moved as quickly as a gazelle.

She raced out the front door with Rodd following her, shouting threats and curses at the top of his lungs. Unfortunately, the fresh air seemed to have revived him because he bore down on her with increasing speed and agility.

Colleen sobbed from pure terror. She had no hopes of outrunning him. It was like trying to keep ahead of a speeding Mack truck; her only recourse was to jump out of its path. She flung open the door of the Ferrari, which was still parked in the driveway, and jumped inside, locking both doors just as his meaty hand closed over the handle.

He tugged hard on the handle, as if he were trying to rip the door off. The car rocked back and forth, but the door held firm. Colleen gave a silent prayer of thanks to the manufacturers, whose road tests couldn't have anticipated such a challenge.

"It's mine!" Rodd yelled, and began to pound on the roof. "My car!"

He sounded like a toddler throwing a tantrum, Colleen thought as she huddled within the confines of the car.

"I'll press charges!" Rodd continued to bellow. "You'll have to drive over me to take my car away!"

A tempting idea, but unfortunately, she didn't have the keys. Another wave of panic assailed her. Where were the keys? She remembered that she'd used them to open the front door. Had she left them in the lock? She felt icy cold, then burning hot with fear. If Rodd were to discover them, he could get into the car . . .

For the first time that night, she was thankful that Rodd was so totally, mindlessly intoxicated. He might have the strength and rage of a mad elephant, but he couldn't reason. His alcohol-soaked brain didn't comprehend why she hadn't driven away; it didn't occur to him to search for the keys. He kept pounding on the car, circling it and rattling the door handles, as Colleen trembled inside it.

Time seemed to grind to a paralyzing standstill, so she had no idea how long it was before she heard a sharp horn blast and saw the headlights of a car that pulled into the driveway behind the Ferrari. She looked through the rearview mirror to see Jack get out of his black Firebird. Colleen closed her eyes and hot tears of sheer relief scalded her cheeks.

"Rodd, what's going on?" Jack approached him slowly.

"Jack! You gotta help me!" bawled Rodd. "She's gonna steal my Ferrari." He began another round of pounding and cursing. This time he kicked the fender, too.

Jack peered inside the car and saw Colleen crying in the driver's seat. His lips thinned into a taut line. "Rodd, calm down," he said quietly. "She won't take the car, I won't let her. Now, come into the house so we can figure out a game plan," he added conspiratorially.

"Game plan," Rodd repeated. "Yeah."

Colleen watched the two of them walk into the house. The moment they were inside, she hopped out of the Ferrari and locked herself in Jack's car. And then a ghastly thought struck her. Suppose Jack was in danger? Who could guess what would set off the volatile Rodd Garrett? She tried to marshall her shattered thoughts and plan a rescue attempt.

But Jack emerged unscathed a few minutes later and strode toward the car. Colleen unlocked the door and let him inside. "Oh, Jack!" His nearness unleased another torrent of tears. "It was awful! I've never been so scared in my whole life!"

Jack stared down at her. The light in the car highlighted a reddened swelling on her cheek, her hair was cascading around her shoulders in wild disarray, and her blouse was ripped. He gripped her shoulders. "Colleen, did he—"

"He tried to attack me," Colleen choked out as she sought to wipe away the tears that were streaming down her cheeks. "He hit me—it—it was like he was crazy, Jack. He didn't even know who I was. He thought I was his ex-girlfriend, Belinda."

Jack touched her swollen cheek. There was going to be a bruise; he could already see the faint traces of purple beginning to discolor her ivory skin. "A guy of Garrett's size and strength could have fractured your cheekbone." His voice caught. There was no end to the list of things the drunken, powerfully strong Rodd Garrett could have done to her.

A terrible, white-hot rage engulfed him. "That bastard! I should've knocked his teeth down his throat when I had the chance!" He swung open the door. "I think I'll do it now."

"No! No!" Colleen reached out to grab him. "No fighting! Please, Jack, let's just get out of here. I want to go home." She was crying so hard she could hardly see, but she clutched blindly at his arm, refusing to let go.

Grimly, Jack slammed the door shut and pulled out of the driveway. Colleen blanched when she saw Rodd Garrett push open the front door of his house and stumble outside again.

"What if he follows us?" she whimpered.

"He won't," Jack assured her. "I have his car keys." He patted his coat pocket. "They were in the front door lock. I didn't want him taking his car out on the road and killing somebody."

They drove away, leaving a shouting Rodd Garrett far behind.

Colleen closed her eyes and tried to calm down. She was safe now, she silently repeated. Her body was wracked by shudders and she felt ice cold inside and out. Even her teeth were chattering. "I—I can't stop shaking. I can't seem to get warm." She couldn't stop crying, either.

"It's a nervous reaction. You've had a shock." He turned up the heater and a blast of hot air filled the car. He was clutching the steering wheel so tightly that his knuckles were white. "Colleen, are you sure you're all right?" he asked, his voice low and intense. "I could take you to the hospital and—"

"No! There's no need. Except for my cheek, he didn't hurt me." She choked on a sob.

"Your blouse is torn," Jack said tautly.

Colleen glanced down, noticing the rip for the first time. "But he didn't—he didn't—" she couldn't say the word.

"He didn't rape you, but he did physically assault you." Jack's tone was as brutal as the charge. "You have the bruise to prove it. I think you should press charges against him, Colleen. We can go to the police station right now."

"No! Oh no!" She gasped as a devastating combination of shock, fear, and horror streaked through her, so intermingled that she couldn't begin to separate one from the other. "I just want to go home and forget that tonight ever happened, Jack."

"I want that lowlife punished for what he did to you—and for what he tried to do." His voice rose as he pictured Colleen at the mercy of Rodd Garrett. "No, I want more than to see him punished. Dammit, I want to see him ruined."

"No, Jack, don't, please! I can't stand any more threats or any more anger."

"Every time I think of him scaring you and hitting you . . . ripping your clothes . . ." Jack swallowed. It felt as if a sharp slice of glass was lodged in his throat. "I can't stand the thought of your being hurt, Colleen. It drives me out of my head."

"He was so different from the person I thought he was, Jack," she whispered. "It was weird—as if he had a whole other personality that the alcohol released. He wasn't acting like himself from the time he arrived to pick me up tonight. He'd probably already been drinking, although I didn't know it at the time."

"I know alcohol has a pathological effect on certain personalities, but I never knew it affected Garrett that way," Jack said tightly. "Why the hell did you go out with him, Colleen?"

"Because you don't want me," Colleen blurted out. "And Nicola and Kamal were going out, and I was so lonely. . . . That's why I went out with him. I'm so sorry I did." She brushed away the tears running down her cheeks.

In what seemed like only a few minutes, Jack pulled the Firebird into the driveway of his house. "We're home," he announced, and Colleen looked around her, daring to hope again, to believe. Home. His home. Theirs.

"I sent Nicola and Kamal over to get my things and bring them back to the apartment," she said softly. "You weren't home when they arrived."

"I was at the drugstore, picking up some more pain reliever for the pounding headache I've had since you walked out on me Friday night. When I got back, I noticed all your stuff was gone, but just in case I hadn't, Nicola left me a poison-pen note." Jack got out of the car and imperiously swept her up in his arms.

Colleen made no protest. Her terror had been converted into a wild, abandoned anticipation, and her whole body throbbed with it. She was keyed up and burning with excitement.

Jack carried her directly to the bedroom and set her down on the bed. "Are we back together?" she asked, her heart beating in triple, quadruple, time.

He said nothing, just gave her a measuring look, then left the room, returning momentarily with an envelope. Inside were torn pieces of paper.

"The check?" Colleen guessed at the same moment that he told her it was. "But what about Quentin's threats?" she dared to ask.

"To hell with Quentin's threats. He can't get me fired or keep me from working. All I have to do is to write one column about his plans, and every First Amendment advocate in the country would be all over him. I never once considered knuckling under to him, Colleen."

Jack tossed the bag to her, frowning. "The only reason I brought that check home was because I was furious with you. You didn't tell me the truth about yourself, and I was so damn mad—"

"You were hurt," Colleen corrected, her eyes filling again, even as a soft smile curved the corners of her mouth. She rose up on her knees and inched slowly toward the edge of the bed where he stood. .

"I was enraged," he corrected grimly. "I wanted to punish you." His arms opened wide to enfold her when she drew near. "You know how bad-tempered I can be, Colleen," he said contritely, his lips brushing the top of her head. "Sweetheart, it never occurred to me that you would leave or would even think that I wanted you to leave. You'd never been intimidated by me or my temper in the past, you always stood right up to me. That's one of the reasons we're so well matched. You're strong enough to handle my occasional bouts of nastiness. And they've occurred less and less often since you've been with me. You're so good for me, Colleen. We're good together, in every way."

"I know," she whispered, wrapping herself around him, clinging to him, crying some more, and silently thanking everyone in heaven who was connected to this, their miraculous reconciliation. "Your temper has never scared me, but this was so much more than a simple fight. I thought you had every right to hate me. I knew I was really in the wrong, Jack. I should have told you about the money and the Ramseys long ago. I wanted to, but—"

"I hadn't made it easy for you with all that juvenile crap I spouted about marrying for money." Jack sighed deeply. "I'm sorry, Colleen. The truth is that I was mad, but I never intended to break up with you. I thought we'd have a helluva fight and I'd make you grovel a little—"

"—or maybe a lot?" Colleen interrupted with a tremulous smile.

"You'd only do it a little before you got mad right back at me," Jack informed her with a grin. "But instead of chasing me into the bedroom like you were supposed to, you took off with Nicola. I was fit to be tied. And I waited all weekend for you to call me and beg to come home, but the damn phone never rang once."

"That's funny," Colleen said softly. "I was waiting for you to call me, but when the phone rang, it was my sisters and Quentin and then Rodd Garrett." She saw the shadow darken Jack's face and quickly pressed on, not wanting to discuss Garrett anymore. "I refused to talk to Quentin and my sisters, and Nicola gave them each a stern lecture on my behalf. I'm still upset that they deliberately came between us."

He bent down and kissed her lightly, tenderly, his lips lingering. "I don't blame them for wanting to protect you, sweetheart. I share the same feeling. And I understand that Quentin Ramsey has your best interests at heart. I'll just have to convince them all that I'm in your best interest."

She sighed contentedly. "You *are.* I love you, Jack. For always."

"Care to repeat that in a church, in front of your family and mine, just as soon as we can arrange it?" Jack asked, smiling down at her.

"Oh yes, Jack!"

"I love you so much, Colleen. I didn't think it was possible to love the way I love you. You've changed my whole life, the way I think and feel about things, and all for the better. You're the one and only woman in the world for me."

They kissed, a deep, loving kiss of commitment and possession, which soon escalated into fiery passion, which drove them wild with wanting. They sank down onto the big bed, tugging impatiently at each other's clothes, kissing and caressing, amidst a soft chorus of moans and sighs. Neither could wait, and their joining was rapid and fierce. He filled her, moving strong and hard within her, and she clung to him, enveloping him, loving him, their bodies binding their souls forever.

"I'm going to ask Quentin Ramsey to have his lawyers draw up an ironclad prenuptial agreement stating in no uncertain terms that what is yours stays yours," Jack said much later as they lay together, replete and content in each other's arms.

"I won't sign it," warned Colleen.

"Colleen, of course you'll sign it. You are not marrying a fortune hunter, and I want to reassure your entire family of that fact."

"They'll be reassured when they meet you and see how much we love each other." She propped herself up on one elbow and stared at him sternly. "I'm not an addle-brained little twit who would fall for the wiles of a fortune hunter, Jack. If my family doesn't know that by now, they'll soon find out."

"There's no use debating the issue, honey. You'll sign the agreement and that's that."

She shook her head. "What's mine is ours and what's yours is ours and that's not negotiable."

"Darling, I'm not going to argue with you—"

"Good. Because you'll lose." She grinned teasingly, provocatively.

"Colleen, you're not behaving like a docile, submissive, compliant little—"

"—simpleton? I should hope not!"

Jack gave a lighthearted laugh and pulled her on top of him. "Promise that you never will."

"I promise," she said happily, hugging him, kissing him, loving him with all her heart.

THE EDITOR'S CORNER

What could be more romantic—Valentine's Day and six LOVESWEPT romances all in one glorious month. And I have the great pleasure of writing my first editor's corner. Let me introduce myself: My name is Nita Taublib, and I have worked as an editorial consultant with the Loveswept staff since Loveswept began. As Carolyn is on vacation and Susann is still at home with her darling baby daughter, I have the honor of introducing the fabulous reading treasures we have in store for you. February is a super month for LOVESWEPT!

Deborah Smith's heroes are always fascinating, and in **THE SILVER FOX AND THE RED-HOT DOVE,** LOVESWEPT #450, the mysterious T. S. Audubon is no exception. He is intrigued by the shy Russian woman who accompanies a famous scientist to a party. And he finds himself filled with a desire to help her escape from her keepers! But when Elena Petrovic makes her own desperate escape, she is too terrified to trust him. Could her handsome enigmatic white-haired rescuer be the silver fox of her childhood fantasy, the only man who could set her loose from a hideous captivity, or does he plan to keep her for himself? Mystery and romance are combined in this passionate tale that will move you to tears.

What man could resist having a gorgeous woman as a bodyguard? Well, as Gail Douglas shows in **BANNED IN BOSTON,** LOVESWEPT #451, rugged and powerful Matt Harper never expects a woman to show up when his mother hires a security consultant to protect him after he receives a series of threatening letters. Annie Brentwood is determined to prove that the best protection demands brains, not brawn. But she forgets that she must also protect herself from the shameless, arrogant, and oh-so-male Matt, who finds himself intoxicated and intrigued by her feisty spirit. Annie finds it hard to resist a man who promises her the last word and I guarantee you will find this a hard book to put down.

Patt Bucheister's hero in **TROPICAL STORM,** LOVESWEPT #452, will make your temperature rise to sultry heights as he tries to woo Cass Mason. Wyatt Brodie has vowed to take Cass back to Key West for a reconciliation with her desperately ill mother. He challenges her to face her past, promising to help if she'll let him. Can she dare surrender to the hunger he has ignited in her yearning heart? Wyatt has warned her that once he makes love to her, they can never be just friends, that he'll fight to keep her from leaving the island. Can he claim the woman he's branded with the fire of his need? Don't miss this very touching, very emotional story.

From the sunny, sultry South we move to snowy Denver in **FROM THIS DAY FORWARD,** LOVESWEPT #453, by Joan Elliot Pickart. John-Trevor Payton has been assigned to befriend Paisley Kane to discover if sudden wealth and a reunion with the father she's never known will bring her happiness or despair. When Paisley knocks John-Trevor into a snowdrift and falls into his arms, his once firmly frozen plans for eternal bachelorhood begin to melt. Paisley has surrounded herself with a patchwork family of nutty boarders in her Denver house, and John-Trevor envies the pleasure she gets from the people she cares for. But Paisley fears she must choose between a fortune and the man destined to

(continued)

be hers. Don't miss this wonderful romance—a real treat for the senses!

Helen Mittermeyer weaves another fascinating story of two lovers reunited in **THE MASK**, LOVE-SWEPT #455. When Cas Griffith lost his young bride to a plane crash over Nepal he was full of grief and guilt and anger. He believed he'd never again want a woman as he'd desired Margo, but when he comes face-to-face with the exotic, mysterious T'ang Qi in front of a New York art gallery two years later, he feels his body come to life again—and knows he must possess the artist who seems such an unusual combination of East and West. The reborn love discovered through their suddenly intimate embraces stuns them both as they seek to exorcise the ghosts of past heartbreak with a love that knows the true meaning of forever.

Sandra Chastain's stories fairly sizzle with powerful emotion and true love, and for this reason we are thrilled to bring you **DANNY'S GIRL**, LOVE-SWEPT #454. Katherine Sinclair had found it hard to resist the seductive claim Danny Dark's words had made on her heart when she was seventeen. Danny had promised to meet her after graduation, but he never came, leaving her to face a pregnancy alone. She'd given the baby up for adoption, gone to college, ended up mayor of Dark River, and never heard from Danny again ... until now. Has he somehow discovered that she was raising her son, Mike—their son—now that his adoptive parents had died? Has he returned merely to try to take Mike from her? Danny still makes her burn and ache with a sizzling passion, but once they know the truth about the past, they have to discover if it is love or only memory that has lasted.

(continued)

Katherine longs to show him that they are a family, that the only time she'll ever be happy is in his arms. You won't soon forget this story of two people and their son trying to become a family.

I hope that you enjoy each and every one of these Valentine treats. We've got a great year of reading pleasure in store for you. . . .

Sincerely,

Nita Taublib

Nita Taublib,
Editorial Consultant,
LOVESWEPT
Bantam Books
666 Fifth Avenue
New York, NY 10103

Starting in February . . .

**An exciting,
unprecedented
mass market
publishing program
designed just for
you . . .
and the way you buy
books!**

Over the past few years, the popularity of genre authors has been unprecedented. Their success is no accident, because readers like you demand high levels of quality from your authors and reward them with fierce loyalty.

Now Bantam Books, the foremost English language mass market publisher in the world, takes another giant step in leadership by dedicating the majority of its paperback list to six genre imprints each and every month.

The six imprints that you will see wherever books
are sold are:

SPECTRA.

For five years the premier publisher of science
fiction and fantasy. Now Spectra expands to add
one title to its list each month, a horror novel.

CRIME LINE.

The award-winning imprint of crime and mystery fiction. Crime Line will expand to embrace
even more areas of contemporary suspense.

DOMAIN.

An imprint that consolidates Bantam's domi-
nance in the frontier fiction, historical saga, and
traditional Western markets.

FALCON.

High-tech action, suspense, espionage, and adventure novels will all be found in the Falcon
imprint, along with Bantam's successful Air &
Space and War books.

BANTAM NONFICTION.

A wide variety of commercial nonfiction, including true crime, health and nutrition, sports, reference books . . . and much more

AND NOW IT IS OUR SPECIAL PLEASURE TO INTRODUCE TO YOU THE SIXTH IMPRINT

FANFARE

FANFARE is the showcase for Bantam's popular women's fiction. With spectacular covers and even more spectacular stories. FANFARE presents three novels each month—ranging from historical to contemporary—all with great human emotion, all with great love stories at their heart, all by the finest authors writing in any genre.

FANFARE LAUNCHES IN FEBRUARY (on sale in early January) WITH THREE BREATHTAKING NOVELS . . .

THE WIND DANCER
by Iris Johansen

TEXAS! LUCKY
by Sandra Brown

WAITING WIVES
by Christina Harland

THE WIND DANCER.

From the spellbinding pen of Iris Johansen comes her most lush, dramatic, and emotionally touching romance yet—a magnificent historical about characters whose lives have been touched by the legendary Wind Dancer. A glorious antiquity, the Wind Dancer is a statue of a Pegasus that is encrusted with jewels . . . but whose worth is beyond the value of its precious stones, gold, and artistry. The Wind Dancer's origins are shrouded in the mist of time . . . and only a chosen few can unleash its mysterious powers. But WIND DANCER is, first and foremost, a magnificent love story. Set in Renaissance Italy where intrigues were as intricate as carved cathedral doors and affairs of state were ruled by affairs of the bedchamber. WIND DANCER tells the captivating story of the lovely and indomitable slave Sanchia and the man who bought her on a back street in Florence. Passionate, powerful *condottiere* Lionello Andreas would love Sanchia and endanger her with equal wild abandon as he sought to win back the prized possession of his family, the Wind Dancer.

TEXAS! LUCKY.

Turning her formidable talent for the first time to the creation of a trilogy, Sandra Brown gives readers a family to remember in the Tylers—brothers Lucky and Chase and their "little" sister Sage. In oil-bust country where Texas millionaires are becoming Texas panhandlers, the Tylers are struggling to keep their drilling business from bankruptcy. Each of the TEXAS! novels tells the love story of one member of the family and combines gritty and colorful characters with the fluid and sensual style the author is lauded for!

WAITING WIVES.
By marvelously talented newcomer Christina Harland, WAITING WIVES is the riveting tale of three vastly different women from different countries whose only bond is the fate of their men who are missing in Vietnam. In this unique novel of great human emotion, full of danger, bravery, and romance, Christina Harland brings to the written page what CHINA BEACH and TOUR OF DUTY have brought to television screens. This is a novel of triumph and honor and hope . . . and love.

Rave reviews are pouring in from critics and much-loved authors on FANFARE's novels for February—and for those in months to come. You'll be delighted and enthralled by works by Amanda Quick and Beverly Byrne, Roseanne Bittner and Kay Hooper, Susan Johnson and Nora Roberts . . . to mention only a few of the remarkable authors in the FAN-FARE imprint.

Special authors. Special covers. And very special stories.

Can you hear the flourish of trumpets now . . . the flourish of trumpets announcing that something special is coming?

FANFARE

Brief excerpts of the launch novels along with praise for them is on the following pages.

New York *Times* bestselling authors Catherine Coulter and Julie Garwood praise the advance copy they read of **WIND DANCER:**

"Iris Johansen is a bestselling author for the best of reasons—she's a wonderful storyteller. Sanchia, Lion, Lorenzo, and Caterina will wrap themselves around your heart and move right in. Enjoy, I did!"
   —Catherine Coulter

"So compelling, so unforgettable a page-turner, this enthralling tale could have been written only by Iris Johansen. I never wanted to leave the world she created with Sanchia and Lion at its center."
   —Julie Garwood

In the following brief excerpt you'll see why *Romantic Times* said this about Iris Johansen and **THE WIND DANCER:**

"The formidable talent of Iris Johansen blazes into incandescent brilliance in this highly original, mesmerizing love story."

We join the story as the evil Carpino, who runs a ring of prostitutes and thieves in Florence, is forcing the young heroine Sanchia to "audition" as a thief for the great *condottiere* Lionello, who waits in the piazza with his friend, Lorenzo, observing at a short distance.

"You're late!" Caprino jerked Sanchia into the shadows of the arcade surrounding the piazza.

"It couldn't be helped," Sanchia said breathlessly. "There was an accident . . . and we didn't get finished until the hour tolled . . . and then I had to wait until Giovanni left to take the—"

Caprino silenced the flow of words with an impatient motion of his hand. "There he is." He nodded across the crowded piazza. "The big man in the wine-colored velvet cape listening to the storyteller."

Sanchia's gaze followed Caprino's to the man standing in front of the platform. He was more than big, he was a giant, she thought gloomily. The careless arrogance in the man's stance bespoke perfect confidence in his ability to deal with any circumstances and, if he caught her, he'd probably use his big strong hands to crush her head like a walnut. Well, she was too tired to worry about that now. It had been over thirty hours since she had slept. Perhaps it was just as well she was almost too exhausted to care what happened to her. Fear must not make her as clumsy as she had been yesterday. She was at least glad the giant appeared able to afford to lose a few ducats. The richness of his clothing indicated he must either be a great lord or a prosperous merchant.

"Go." Caprino gave her a little push out onto the piazza. "Now."

She pulled her shawl over her head to shadow her face and hurried toward the platform where a man was telling a story, accompanying himself on the lyre.

A drop of rain struck her face, and she glanced up at the suddenly dark skies. Not yet, she thought with exasperation. If it started to rain in earnest the people crowding the piazza would run for shelter and she would have to follow the velvet-clad giant until he put himself into a situation that allowed her to make the snatch.

Another drop splashed her hand, and her anxious gaze flew to the giant. His attention was still fixed on the storyteller, but only the saints knew how long he would remain engrossed. This storyteller was not very good. Her pace quickened as she flowed like a shadow into the crowd surrounding the platform.

Garlic, Lion thought, as the odor assaulted his nostrils. Garlic, spoiled fish, and some other stench that smelled even fouler. He glanced around the crowd trying to identify the source of the smell. The people surrounding the platform were the same ones he had studied moments before, trying to search out Caprino's thief. The only new arrival was a thin woman dressed in a shabby gray gown, an equally ragged woolen shawl covering her head.

She moved away from the edge of the crowd and started to hurry across the piazza. The stench faded with her departure and Lion drew a deep breath. *Dio*, luck was with him in this, at least. He was not at all pleased at being forced to stand in the rain waiting for Caprino to produce his master thief.

"It's done," Lorenzo muttered, suddenly at Lion's side. He had been watching from the far side of the crowd. Now he said more loudly, "As sweet a snatch as I've ever seen."

"What?" Frowning, Lion gazed at him. "There was no—" He broke off as he glanced down at his belt. The pouch was gone; only the severed cords remained in his belt. "Sweet Jesus." His gaze flew around the piazza. "Who?"

"The sweet madonna who looked like a beggar maid and smelled like a decaying corpse." Lorenzo nodded toward the arched arcade. "She disappeared behind that column, and I'll wager you'll find Caprino lurking there with her, counting your ducats."

Lion started toward the column. "A woman," he murmured. "I didn't expect a woman. How good is she?"

Lorenzo fell into step with him. "Very good."

Iris Johansen's fabulous romances of characters whose lives are touched by the Wind Dancer go on! STORM WINDS, coming from FANFARE in June 1991, is another historical. REAP THE WIND, a contemporary, will be published by FANFARE in November 1991.

Sandra Brown, whose legion of fans catapulted her last contemporary novel onto the *New York Times* list, has received the highest praise in advance reviews of **TEXAS! LUCKY**. *Rave Reviews* said, "Romance fans will relish all of Ms. Brown's provocative sensuality along with a fast-paced plotline that springs one surprise after another. Another feast for the senses from one of the world's hottest pens."

Indeed Sandra's pen is "hot"—especially so in her incredible **TEXAS!** trilogy. We're going to peek in on an early episode in which Lucky has been hurt in a brawl in a bar where he was warding off the attentions of two town bullies toward a redhead he hadn't met, but wanted to get to know very well.

This woman was going to be an exciting challenge, something rare that didn't come along every day. Hell, he'd never had anybody exactly like her.

"What's your name?"

She raised deep forest-green eyes to his. "D-D Dovey."

" 'D-D Dovey'?"

"That's right," she snapped defensively. "What's wrong with it?"

"Nothing. I just hadn't noticed your stuttering before. Or has the sight of my bare chest made you develop a speech impediment?"

"Hardly. Mr.—?"

"Lucky."

"Mr. Lucky?"

"No, I'm Lucky."

"Why is that?"

"I mean my name is Lucky. Lucky Tyler."

"Oh. Well. I assure you the sight of your bare chest leaves me cold, Mr. Tyler."

He didn't believe her and the smile that tilted up one corner of his mouth said so. "Call me Lucky."

She reached for the bottle of whiskey on the nightstand and raised it in salute. "Well, Lucky, your luck just ran out."

"Huh?"

"Hold your breath." Before he could draw a sufficient one, she tipped the bottle and drizzled the liquor over the cut.

He blasted the four walls with words unfit to be spoken aloud, much less shouted. "Oh hell, oh—"

"Your language isn't becoming to a gentleman, Mr. Tyler."

"I'm gonna murder you. Stop pouring that stuff— Agh!"

"You're acting like a big baby."

"What the hell are you trying to do, scald me?"

"Kill the germs."

"Damn! It's killing *me.* Do something. Blow on it."

"That only causes germs to spread."

"Blow on it!"

She bent her head over his middle and blew gently along the cut. Her breath fanned his skin and cooled the stinging whiskey in the open wound. Droplets of it had collected in the satiny stripe of hair beneath his navel. Rivulets trickled beneath the waistband of his jeans. She blotted at them with her fingertips, then, without thinking, licked the liquor off her own skin. When she realized what she'd done, she sprang upright. "Better now?" she asked huskily.

When Lucky's blue eyes connected with hers, it was like completing an electric circuit. The atmosphere crackled. Matching her husky tone of voice, he said, "Yeah, much better. . . . Thanks," he mumbled. Her hand felt so comforting and cool, the way his mother's always had whenever he was sick with fever. He captured Dovey's hand with his and pressed it against his hot cheek.

She withdrew it and, in a schoolmarm's voice, said, "You can stay only until the swelling goes down."

"I don't think I'll be going anywhere a-tall tonight," he said. "I feel like hell. This is all I want to do. Lie here. Real still and quiet."

Through a mist of pain, he watched her remove her jacket and drape it over the back of a chair. Just as he'd thought—quite a looker was Dovey. But that wasn't all. She looked like a woman who knew her own mind and wasn't afraid to speak it. Levelheaded.

So what the hell had she been doing in that bar?

He drifted off while puzzling through the question.

Now on sale in DOUBLEDAY hardcover is the next in Sandra's fantastic trilogy, TEXAS! CHASE, about which *Rendezvous* has said: ". . . it's the story of a love that is deeper than the oceans, and more lasting than the land itself. Lucky's story was fantastic; Chase's story is more so." FANFARE's paperback of TEXAS! CHASE will go on sale August 1991.

Rather than excerpt from the extraordinary novel **WAITING WIVES**, which focuses on three magnificent women, we will describe the book in some detail. The three heroines whom you'll love and root for give added definition to the words growth and courage . . . and love.

ABBRA is talented and sheltered, a raven-haired beauty who was just eighteen when she fell rapturously in love with handsome Army captain Lewis Ellis. Immediately after their marriage he leaves for Vietnam. Passionately devoted to Lewis, she lives for his return—until she's told he's dead. Then her despair turns to torment as she falls hopelessly in love with Lewis's irresistible brother. . . .

SERENA never regrets her wildly impulsive marriage to seductive Kyle Anderson. But she does regret her life of unabashed decadence and uninhibited pleasure—especially when she discovers a dirty, bug-infested orphanage in Saigon . . . and Kyle's illegitimate child.

GABRIELLE is the daughter of a French father and a Vietnamese mother. A flame-haired singer with urchin appeal and a sultry voice, she is destined for stardom. But she gives her heart—and a great part of her future—to a handsome Aussie war correspondent. Gavin is determined to record the "real" events of the Vietnam war . . . but his search for truth leads him straight into the hands of the Viet Cong and North Vietnamese, who have no intention of letting him report anything until they've won the war.

Christina Harland is an author we believe in. Her story is one that made all of us who work on FANFARE cry, laugh, and turn pages like mad. We predict that WAITING WIVES will fascinate and enthrall you . . . and that you will say with us, "it is a novel whose time has come."

We hope you will greet FANFARE next month with jubilation! It is an imprint we believe you will delight in month after month, year after year to come.

THE "VIVE LA ROMANCE" SWEEPSTAKES

Don't miss your chance to speak to your favorite Loveswept authors on the LOVESWEPT LINE 1-900-896-2505*

You may win a glorious week for two in the world's most romantic city, Paris, France by entering the "Vive La Romance" sweepstakes when you call. With travel arrangements made by Reliable Travel, you and that special someone will fly American Airlines to Paris, where you'll be guests at the famous Lancaster Hotel. Why not call right now? Your own Loveswept fantasy could come true!

Official Rules:

Official Rules cont'd

2. 1 Grand Prize: A vacation trip for two to Paris, France for 7 nights. Trip includes accommodations at the deluxe Lancaster Hotel and round-trip coach tickets to Paris on American Airlines from the American Airlines airport nearest the winner's residence which provides direct service to New York.
(Approximate Retail Value: $3,500).

3. Sweepstakes begins October 1, 1990 and all entries must be received by December 31, 1990. All entrants must be 18 years of age or older at the time of entry. The winner will be chosen by Bantam's Marketing Department by a random drawing to be held on or about January 15, 1991 from all entries received and will be notified by mail. Bantam's decision is final. The winner has 30 days from date of notice in which to accept the prize award or an alternate winner will be chosen. The prize is not transferable and no substitution is allowed. The trip must be taken by November 22, 1991, and is subject to airline departure schedules and ticket and accommodation availability. Certain blackout periods may apply. Winner must have a valid passport. Odds of winning depend on the number of entries received. Enter as often as you wish, but each mail-in entry must be entered separately. No mechanically reproduced entries allowed.

4. The winner and his or her guest will be required to execute an Affidavit of Eligibility and Promotional Release supplied by Bantam. Entering the sweepstakes constitutes permission for use of winner's name, address and likeness for publicity and promotional purposes, with no additional compensation or permission.

5. This sweepstakes is open only to residents of the U.S. who are 18 years of age or older, and is void in Puerto Rico and wherever else prohibited or restricted by law. Employees of Bantam Books, Bantam Doubleday Dell Publishing Group, Inc., Reliable Travel, Call Interactive, their subsidiaries and affiliates, and their immediate family members are not eligible to enter this sweepstakes. Taxes, if any, are the winner's sole responsibility.

6. Bantam is the sole sponsor of the sweepstakes. Bantam reserves the right to cancel the sweepstakes via the 900 number at any time and without prior notice, but entry into the sweepstakes via mail through December 31, 1990 will remain. Bantam is not responsible for lost, delayed or misdirected entries, and Bantam, Call Interactive, and AT&T are not responsible for any error, incorrect or inaccurate entry of information by entrants, malfunctions of the telephone network, computer equipment software or any combination thereof. This Sweepstakes is subject to the complete Official Rules.

7. For the name of the prize winner (available after January 15, 1991), send a stamped, self-addressed envelope entirely separate from your entry to:

VIVE LA ROMANCE SWEEPSTAKES WINNER LIST,
Bantam Books, Dept. CK-3, 666 Fifth Avenue,
New York, New York 10103.

Loveswept ®

60 Minutes to a Better, More Beautiful You!

Now it's easier than ever to awaken your sensuality, stay slim forever—even make yourself irresistible. With Bantam's bestselling subliminal audio tapes, you're only 60 minutes away from a better, more beautiful you!

__ 45004-2	**Slim Forever**	$8.95
__ 45112-X	**Awaken Your Sensuality**	$7.95
__ 45035-2	**Stop Smoking Forever**	$8.95
__ 45130-8	**Develop Your Intuition**	$7.95
__ 45022-0	**Positively Change Your Life**	$8.95
__ 45154-5	**Get What You Want**	$7.95
__ 45041-7	**Stress Free Forever**	$8.95
__ 45106-5	**Get a Good Night's Sleep**	$7.95
__ 45094-8	**Improve Your Concentration**	$7.95
__ 45172-3	**Develop A Perfect Memory**	$8.95

THE LATEST IN BOOKS
AND AUDIO CASSETTES

Paperbacks

☐	28671	**NOBODY'S FAULT** Nancy Holmes	$5.95
☐	28412	**A SEASON OF SWANS** Celeste De Blasis	$5.95
☐	28354	**SEDUCTION** Amanda Quick	$4.50
☐	28594	**SURRENDER** Amanda Quick	$4.50
☐	28435	**WORLD OF DIFFERENCE** Leonia Blair	$5.95
☐	28416	**RIGHTFULLY MINE** Doris Mortman	$5.95
☐	27032	**FIRST BORN** Doris Mortman	$4.95
☐	27283	**BRAZEN VIRTUE** Nora Roberts	$4.50
☐	27891	**PEOPLE LIKE US** Dominick Dunne	$4.95
☐	27260	**WILD SWAN** Celeste De Blasis	$5.95
☐	25692	**SWAN'S CHANCE** Celeste De Blasis	$5.95
☐	27790	**A WOMAN OF SUBSTANCE** Barbara Taylor Bradford	$5.95

Audio

☐ **SEPTEMBER** by Rosamunde Pilcher
Performance by Lynn Redgrave
180 Mins. Double Cassette   45241-X $15.95

☐ **THE SHELL SEEKERS** by Rosamunde Pilcher
Performance by Lynn Redgrave
180 Mins. Double Cassette   48183-9 $14.95

☐ **COLD SASSY TREE** by Olive Ann Burns
Performance by Richard Thomas
180 Mins. Double Cassette   45166-9 $14.95

☐ **NOBODY'S FAULT** by Nancy Holmes
Performance by Geraldine James
180 Mins. Double Cassette   45250-9 $14.95